THE BILLIONAIRE DEAL

THE SUTTON BILLIONAIRES SERIES, BOOK 1

LORI RYAN

Copyright 2020, Lori Ryan.

All rights reserved.

This book contains material protected under International and Federal Copyright Laws and Treaties. Any unauthorized reprint or use of this material is prohibited. No part of this book may be reproduced or transmitted in any form or by any means, electronic or mechanical, including photocopying, recording, or by any information storage and retrieval system without express written permission from the author/publisher.

ISBN: 978-1-941149-97-3

OTHER BOOKS BY LORI RYAN

The Sutton Billionaires Series:

The Billionaire Deal

Reuniting with the Billionaire

The Billionaire Op

The Billionaire's Rock Star

The Billionaire's Navy SEAL

Falling for the Billionaire's Daughter

The Sutton Capital Intrigue Series:

Cutthroat

Cut and Run

Cut to the Chase

The Sutton Capital on the Line Series:

Pure Vengeance

Latent Danger

The Triple Play Curse Novellas:

Game Changer

Game Maker

Game Clincher

The Heroes of Evers, TX Series:

Love and Protect

Promise and Protect

Honor and Protect (An Evers, TX Novella)

Serve and Protect

Desire and Protect

Cherish and Protect

Treasure and Protect

The Dark Falls, CO Series:

Dark Falls

Dark Burning

Dark Prison

Coming Soon – The Halo Security Series:

Dulce's Defender

Hannah's Hero

Shay's Shelter

Callie's Cover

Grace's Guardian

Sophie's Sentry

Sienna's Sentinal

For the most current list of Lori's books, visit her website: loriryanromance.com.

ACKNOWLEDGMENTS

Thank you to my wonderful husband for his patience and support. Thank you to Susan Smith for her endless brainstorming and reading, and to Cathy Cobb, Amy Glasgow, and Liz Burton for reading early drafts. Thank you to Patricia Thomas whose editing proved invaluable, and to Bev Harrison who helped me release an updated version of this book in 2013. Thank you to Patricia Parent, my final set of eyes, for cleaning up after me. Thank you to all of the friends and friends-of-friends who read the pre-release version for me. I owe you all so much.

Thank you to all of my amazing Lori's Lilacs who proofread this new version for me! Your support humbles me.

AUTHOR'S NOTE

If you love *The Billionaire Deal* and want to read more about the lives of the people at Sutton Capital, send me your email and I'll send you *Reuniting with the Billionaire*, book two in the Sutton Billionaires Series, free!

CHAPTER 1

Whish, swoosh, whish, swoosh, whish, swoosh.
Jack Sutton lost himself in the rhythmic sound of the churning wheels of his bike as he rounded the final bend of an eight-mile morning ride.

He was flanked by his cousin, Chad, who was more like a brother to him than a cousin, and their best friend, Andrew. The three met once or twice a month to ride next to the Long Island Sound where Jack's home was located.

Jack saw Chad soar past him out of the corner of his eye as he raced the last few yards ahead of him and Andrew, cutting into Jack's driveway to easily take the lead. It never ceased to amaze Jack.

Chad had a good three inches over Jack's tall frame, and he was built like a military tank. The man shouldn't be able to move the way he did, but he was still somehow faster and more agile than both Andrew and Jack.

Jack and Andrew exchanged a look, grinning at Chad's need to beat them every time they rode. Most days, Andrew and Jack would at least give Chad a fight over the winning slot, but beating Chad wasn't on Jack's mind today, and he had a feeling it wasn't on Andrew's either.

The showdown he would have with Chad's mother—Jack's Aunt Mabry—later today was what had him tense and uneasy. He had hoped the morning ride would take the edge off, but it hadn't helped.

He shoved aside his mood long enough to put on a show for Chad while the three men rode slow laps through the circular drive to cool down, each one sipping water and talking trash as they rode. He'd be damned if he'd let Chad see anything was wrong. He wouldn't make his cousin choose a side no matter what Mabry threw at him.

It wasn't until after Chad loaded up his bike and pulled out of the driveway that Jack raised the subject they'd been avoiding for the last couple of hours.

"Spill it," Jack said. Andrew had been grinding his jaw the whole ride, so he knew whatever he'd been avoiding saying in front of Chad wasn't good.

Andrew was one of a handful of people who knew Chad's mother was finally making good on her threat to try to take over the company Jack's father had built. The terms of Jack's mother's will were going to let her take control of a large portion of the shares of Sutton Capital, and vote Jack out of his position as Chief Executive Officer.

She wanted Chad to take Jack's place at the head of the board table and she was willing to do whatever it took to see that happen.

Jack and Andrew had been quietly approaching the shareholders in the privately-owned company to be sure Jack had their support if Mabry got her hands on the stock his mother had once controlled.

Andrew didn't blink when he looked at Jack and broke the news. "John Barton died of a heart attack last night."

Jack swallowed a curse and swiped his face with his hand. "He wasn't very old at all. When did it happen?" he asked, shock hitting him like a sledge hammer.

"Sixty-seven and supposed to be retired, but he didn't know the definition of the word. I don't think the man has taken a vacation in twenty years, but Anne finally talked him into going to Italy. They were supposed to leave in three days for a two-week vacation and then this happens."

The two men were silent for a few minutes before Jack realized what this meant for his battle with Mabry.

Oh hell. He scrubbed a hand down his face. This could not be happening. "I know this isn't a great time to bring this up, but— " Jack began before Andrew cut in.

"But nothing. You have to think about the rest of the shareholders, the company, its employees—there's a lot at stake for a lot of people here, Jack. We need to figure out who will have control of Barton's shares, and find out what that does to our chances against your Aunt Mabry."

This time Jack didn't bother to swallow his curse. He let fly with a few words his mother would have been pissed to hear coming from his mouth.

"Grab a shower and meet me at the office," he said. "We'll deal with this there." He didn't wait for an answer. He turned and took the front steps two at a time, hustling to get showered and dressed to deal with the latest catastrophe in his ongoing battle with his aunt.

CHAPTER 2

Kelly Bradley pulled into the parking lot of her condo complex and shut off her car. Grabbing three bags of groceries from the trunk, she headed for the stairs but went right at the top instead of toward her own condo on the left. She raised her fist and pounded. Hard.

"Mr. Anders! Mr. Anders!" she called loudly through the door. "It's Kelly. From next door."

Kelly stopped and waited. And waited. She knew it would take Mr. Anders a little while to work his way to the door. His car was in the parking lot and he wasn't much of a walker, so chances were he was home.

While she waited, Kelly propped her grocery bags against the wall next to her doorway and pulled out the cookies she'd bought for her neighbor. The door behind her opened. She turned to find the slender white-haired man smiling at her with a mouth that was now fairly devoid of teeth.

"Hello, dear!" the old man bellowed, but it came out more like "hewwo deah" due to the lack of teeth.

His hearing had gone long before his teeth had. They compensated by hollering at one another most of the time.

Whenever it snowed, Mr. Anders always managed to beat her

downstairs to the parking lot. He'd clean off his car and then do hers. He scraped the ice from the windows before she even made it out of bed. Since he wouldn't stop doing it even though she insisted he didn't need to, Kelly had taken to bringing him occasional treats as a way of saying thank you. It was summer now, but she saw no reason to stop just because the snow was gone.

"Hi, Mr. Anders!" she shouted back as she handed him the box of cookies. "I got you cookies since I was at the store."

"You got me cookies from a whore?" he yelled back with a puzzled look on his face. Kelly felt her cheeks burn red and she sputtered, trying to figure out what to say.

Within seconds, her neighbor cracked a grin. "Gotcha," he said and slapped his leg as he laughed. "Can you come in for a cookie?"

Kelly laughed, but the red spots stayed high on her cheeks as she shook her head at the incorrigible man. "Sorry, Mr. Anders. I'm meeting a friend for lunch so I've got to run. I'll stop by soon though."

He was still laughing when he shut his door. Kelly whipped into her place, unpacked the refrigerated and frozen items in her grocery bags, shoving it haphazardly into any empty space she could find.

She wanted to run to her mailbox before heading to lunch. With any luck, she'd get the final few envelopes she'd been waiting for today.

She crossed the lawn to the large bank of mailboxes that served the entire complex. The letters arriving today would make or break Kelly's dream.

CHAPTER 3

An hour later, Jack stalked through the lobby of his New Haven office building with his jaw clenched. His scowl wasn't aimed at anyone or anything in particular on his way up to the 26th floor offices of Sutton Capital, but people moved out of his way.

He stabbed "26" on the elevator control panel and thought about the unpleasant conversation he and Andrew were about to have. It wouldn't be fun trying to figure out how a man's death would affect this vote, but they didn't have a choice right now. The clock was ticking thanks to the terms of his mother's will.

Ding. The elevator doors slid open to reveal the reception desk and waiting area of Jack's company. A deep burgundy carpet with gray edging set the tone for the company as luxurious, professional, and successful. The plush leather chairs and polished petrified wood end tables told anyone entering the space that Sutton Capital was no small-time company. Just the way Jack liked.

His nod to the receptionist was curt but polite as he moved past her toward his corner office.

Jennie looked up when he stopped in front of her desk before entering his office. She was a temp who'd taken over when his own secretary had to leave suddenly for a family crisis, but she'd been more than competent so far.

She always seemed to know when he needed something and she was a whiz at organizing large quantities of data and pulling together what he needed to see quickly.

He might tell HR they could go ahead and hire her on permanently if there was room for her anywhere in the company.

"Jennie, Andrew will be here in a few minutes. Show him right in when he arrives." He started to turn away, but turned back. "Will you ask Roark to join us when he gets in?"

"Yes, Mr. Sutton," Jennie said with a nod.

Roark Walker was head of Sutton's legal department, but he had also been friends with Jack's mother and father. Jack was still holding out hope the man would have some last-minute solution for this cluster of a situation that was threatening to derail the company he'd thought he would lead for, well forever if he was honest with himself.

Jack strode to his office and shut the door, pacing as he waited for Andrew to arrive. Andrew wasn't just his best friend; he was also the Chief Financial Officer of Sutton Capital and Jack's right-hand man at the company.

He hoped Andrew would have good news to help him out of this colossal mess. Andrew was one of the few people that knew Jack the man, beyond Jack the CEO of Sutton Capital. They went far enough back that neither saw the other the way their adversaries did.

Jack's business rivals feared him and his investors respected him, at least insofar as they knew he could make them a hell of a lot of money.

He never felt weak or anxious when he stepped up to the negotiating table, and he normally thrived on stress and pressure. But, on this—possibly the biggest deal of his life—the unique circumstances had him feeling as if he had maneuvered and negotiated himself right into a corner.

He moved to his mahogany desk and stared down at his reflection in its uncluttered surface. His plans had fallen apart. He had been so certain his strategy would work that he'd become overconfident. That wasn't like him at all. Jack knew it was his late mother's involvement in his current situation that had thrown him off his game. He had loved his mom so he hadn't wanted to address the terms of her will head on and try to challenge her, even if she was no longer here to see him do it.

Now he'd screwed himself over. He needed to come up with another plan and execute it quickly if he was going to save his position in the family company.

When Jennie opened the door and ushered Andrew inside, the tight line of his friend's lips told Jack things hadn't gone as they'd hoped.

Andrew had been in on his plan from the beginning. He was Jack's closest confidant and supporter, but right now it didn't look like his friend had the news they needed.

"Thank you, Jennie. Hold my calls," he directed.

"Yes, sir." Jennie closed the door behind her, leaving the two men in silence.

CHAPTER 4

*J*ennie rushed back to her desk to turn on her intercom. As a temp secretary, she took a lot of liberties she might not take if her job were more secure but she'd been told there was no chance for this position to become permanent. Jack Sutton's secretary would be back in a week.

Early on at Sutton Capital, she discovered the indicator light on the intercom between Jack's office and her desk didn't light up when it should, leaving him with no way to know if she'd activated it from her end of the line. She'd been listening in on conversations ever since and she wasn't about to pass up listening in on this one. She had no doubt this would be juicy.

Yesterday, she'd heard Jack's aunt threatening to take over the company and put her son in charge. From what she could gather, when Mr. Sutton's mother passed away five years ago, she'd held the largest single chunk of shares in the company—at thirty-five percent. The remaining shares of the privately held company were owned in varying amounts by the six members of the board of directors, including Jack.

But Mr. Sutton's mother was apparently a romantic who cared more about her son's marital status than the state of the family business. She placed her shares in a trust, with Jack holding the proxy voting rights.

If Jack wasn't married by the time he was thirty-five, the trust remained in place, but the proxy rights reverted to his Aunt Mabry. Yesterday, Mabry told him she was going to use the strength of those shares to make a bid for Chad to take Jack's place as CEO.

For some reason that wasn't clear in the conversation Jennie overheard, Mabry wanted to hurt Jack.

If he wanted to stay in his position as CEO, Jack either needed to have enough board members on his side to know he could win a vote…or he needed to get married before he turned thirty-five. Next week.

If Jack was married, the shares his mother left in trust would become Jack's outright. Mabry wouldn't be able to touch him.

In the two months Jennie had filled in as secretary for Jack Sutton, she'd heard no mention of a fiancée or even a serious girlfriend, so she'd almost fallen out of her chair when she heard Jack tell his aunt he planned to marry his fiancée at the end of the week.

If you believed the tabloids, Jack Sutton had a different woman on his arm every week. Jennie could imagine most of them were hoping to be the one for him.

She smirked. The one to take his wallet and run away with it. She would bet that most women saw his money, his cars, the bank accounts that had to total in the billions and all think they could be the one to spend it all for him.

So, yeah, it had been a bit of a surprise when he'd said he was marrying one of them. When his aunt pressed for a name, he was vague and told her she could drop by the next afternoon to meet his fiancée.

As Jennie listened in on Jack's meeting with Andrew, Jennie finally figured out why he'd told his aunt such a flat-out lie.

CHAPTER 5

"Not good news?" Jack knew from the look on Andrew's face he didn't have anything but bad news.

"Barton's death put a real kink in things for us. He held eight percent of the shares. Mabry holds ten percent. It seems that John's shares were left to his son, Bryan. I made some calls to try to find out more about the son so we can figure out how he'll vote, but I can't be certain yet."

Andrew didn't have to tell Jack that was bad news. Bryan didn't like Jack. It was stupid really, but it was what it was.

Andrew went on. "It turns out that Bryan Barton went to school with Chad. What I haven't been able to find out is whether they were friends, enemies, or indifferent," Andrew reported.

"It won't matter," Jack said. "Bryan doesn't like me."

Andrew's brows went up.

"I brought a woman to a charity event once. I don't remember her name. Vivian or Vixen, something like that." He waved a hand. "Turns out they had been dating. She wanted a proposal and he wasn't moving fast enough, so she hit on me thinking she could make him jealous and back him into a corner. I needed a date that weekend."

Jack shrugged. She'd been nothing more than a woman on

his arm for the night. Honestly he wasn't even sure if they'd had sex afterward.

But she'd been more than that to Bryan. He hadn't gotten over that. He'd been cold to Jack since then, which was ridiculous since it wasn't like they were in high school. Hell, even if they had been in high school, Jack would have thought the grudge was ridiculous.

Andrew shook his head. "If Bryan votes with Mabry, and she has her shares plus control of the proxy shares—they'll have a small majority."

Jack leaned back in his chair and let out a frustrated growl. "This is a nightmare. How is it all falling apart at the last minute? If we don't have Bryan on our side, she can push me out."

He looked to his friend. "I know it's wrong to talk about a man's death like this, but the timing couldn't be worse. It's not the money that matters to me." He didn't really need to tell Andrew that, but he did.

Jack had been more than comfortable before he took over Sutton Capital, having inherited a chunk of money from his grandfather and more from his parents when they passed.

At this point, though, saying Jack was comfortable didn't begin to cover it. He was stupid rich. Andrew had helped Jack wisely invest his inheritance and the money he had earned over the years. Jack had more than enough money to last him ten lifetimes, whether he worked another day in his life or not. This wasn't about the money.

"My grandfather and dad started this company from the ground up. I've done a damn good job expanding it, too," Jack said, crossing his arms as if he dared Andrew or anyone else to deny the assertion. He was proud of the way his dad had trusted him with the company, and proud of what he'd done to grow it in the time he'd been in charge.

"I know. We all do. That's why any of the existing board members would have voted for you. Your risky decisions pay off even when they shouldn't and people trust your judgment. But, Bryan Barton is a wild card. We can't predict what he'll do." Andrew shook his head. He leaned forward, his forearms resting on his thighs. He looked at his longtime friend. "I guess you're going to have to get married, bro."

Jack grunted. "I'm not getting married. I like my life the way it is," Jack said.

Even as he said it, he knew on some level he was lying to himself.

He would kill to have what his mom and dad had when they were alive; his parents shared a love so powerful, it lasted until the day they died.

He'd yet to come close to that with any of the women he dated.

Andrew sat quietly and let Jack vent. The ability to do so was one of Andrew's strengths—knowing when to be quiet and wait out a storm. Jack knew there really wasn't anything his friend could say for the moment, but it helped to gripe.

"I'm perfectly happy living as a bachelor. I don't know why my mom couldn't understand that. Just because they had a great marriage doesn't mean that's the only way I'll be happy, does it? Well, does it?"

Yeah, it does, thought Jack, but forced that thought out of his mind. He had never met anyone who made him feel the way he knew his mother and father felt together, so he was careful not to let those hopes surface anymore.

Andrew remained silent but shook his head.

Jack knew he sounded more like a toddler than the CEO of a multimillion-dollar corporation, but he had come to realize a long time ago he wasn't cut out to have the kind of love his parents had found. Being forced to marry to save his company sent his mood into a downward spiral.

A knock sounded on the door and Roark Walker poked his head in the door, entering when Jack waved him in.

Roark had been good friends with his mother and father. The tall man had hair that had gone white that he kept cropped close to his head and deep brown skin that never seemed to wrinkle or age despite his sixty years.

"You holding up?" Roark asked as he sank into the other seat in front of Jack's desk and nodded a greeting to Andrew.

Jack shot him a look. "I'm about to lose my company because I haven't fallen in love. Happy birthday to me."

Roark gave a little shrug. "There are worse things."

Jack could only stare at the man. Sure, there was cancer and car accidents and shit like that, but was the man really telling him there were worse things than losing control of the company that was your life?

"Can we challenge the will? Maybe get an emergency stay keeping my aunt from exercising her rights to the votes." Jack had to try something. He wouldn't just sit back and let her take his company away from him.

Roark shook his head. "When your mom told me what she wanted to put in her will, I sent her to a friend of mine who does trusts and estate work to write up the trust. It's solid, Jack. You're not going to get around that."

"If I can get an injunction I can figure something out. I could have someone try to buy Bryan's shares. He doesn't need to know it's me."

Roark was shaking his head. "Jack, your mom wanted to see you married. She wanted you to find the happiness she and your father had."

"What are you saying I should do? Run out and find someone to marry in five days?" He wanted to hit something. Or throw shit. Here he'd been claiming he wasn't going to have the kind of outburst he might have in high school, but he was going to lose control if he didn't get this shit in check fast.

"I'm saying maybe it wouldn't be a bad thing for you to step back from the company." Roark raised his hands in surrender when Jack's look went from dark to downright black. "I'm only saying, your mom saw the way you've made this company your everything, made it your life. She didn't want that for you. Maybe you need to honor that."

Jack slammed his hands down on the desk. "Fuck!"

His mom just hadn't understood that he wasn't like her and his dad. For one thing, they'd fallen in love before his family had made all their money. Neither one of them had to wonder if that person was with them for their money.

Jack was so lost in the emotions roiling through his gut he barely noticed when Roark slipped from the room leaving Andrew and Jack alone again.

"We can gamble that your aunt won't be able to get the swing votes she needs or we can go to Chad and ask him to step in and stop her. Nobody's even asked him if he wants to be the CEO. Honestly, I think it's time to ask." Andrew suggested.

Jack ran his hands through his hair and leaned back in his chair to think. He stayed that way for a few moments and then sat up and turned back toward Andrew before speaking.

"Chad's never mentioned anything to me that makes me think he'd want a shot at being in charge, but he's competitive. You know that. And I don't want to ask him to choose between his mom and me. I know it's hard for you to understand, but I remember what my Aunt Mabry was like before her husband walked out on her. You can't see it now because she's so filled with hate, but she wasn't like that when I was growing up. Hell, I once loved her as much as I loved my own mom. When my uncle left her, she cracked.

"Hell, Chad might side with her which pits me against him. And if Chad stands up to her and sides with me, she'll think he's abandoning her too. I can't do that to her. I know it's crazy, but I can't." Jack crossed to the window on the other side of his office and stared at the view of the Yale campus. His commitment to what was left of his family warred with his drive to protect his position as CEO.

"I still don't understand why she's focused on hurting you," Andrew said as he shook his head.

Jack sighed. "She went after my dad before me. When my uncle left her, she wasn't able to lash out at him because he just took off. He left her almost all their money and Chad was an adult, so custody wasn't an issue. There was no fight she could throw her anger into. I think she needed to lash out at someone and my parents were happily married. That seemed to make her angry so she began to attack them. Now that they're gone, she's moved on to me." He shrugged, knowing his aunt's anger made no more sense than his need to protect her in the face of it.

"All right, but let's walk through this. Even if she gets the board to vote you out, we can try to convince Chad to refuse the position. He might." Andrew reasoned.

"Even if he does, at that point, the board's confidence in me will be shot. If my own aunt takes me out, they'll question my ability, so even if Chad refuses the position, they'll go outside for a new CEO instead of coming back to me. And, even if none of that happens, if she has the proxy rights, she can make every decision that comes before the board into a battle. We have a great board right now with really sharp people. We work well together. She'd tear this board apart if she had those voting rights, and the company could crumble given enough time."

Jack couldn't see any way around the mess he was in. And he knew he didn't want to ask Chad to make this choice.

He laughed, the realization of what he'd told his aunt hitting him. "I told Mabry I was getting married, for God's sake. She'll be here at three o'clock to meet my fiancée. Hell, I thought I was just buying time. If I don't have those votes..."

There was no humor in his laughter, only frustration and disbelief that something like this could have happened without him getting out ahead of it.

He was always ten steps ahead. *Always.*

"That's three hours from now. Let me see if I can find out which way Bryan might vote or come up with something else. I tried tracking down Chad earlier so I could casually mention Bryan and see if they were friends, but I haven't been able to reach him since he left your house this morning." Andrew said.

"Okay. Let's work the problem. We can't exactly call Bryan Barton and ask what his vote would be since he's burying his father tomorrow. If the man wasn't still holding a grudge against me, he would if we pulled that shit. But, let's try to talk to other alumni we know to see if Barton and Chad were tight in school. And, keep looking for Chad to see what you can get out of him without letting him know what's going on."

"Why not tell him what's going on?"

Jack shrugged. "Why tell him if I don't want him to solve the problem?"

"Maybe he'll have an idea. Another way out?"

"Can't chance that." Jack turned back to his desk. "He'll want to go to his mom, and I'm not ready for that."

"I'll let you know what I come up with. In the meantime, start running through your little black book and figure out which of your booty calls may be looking for something more permanent," Andrew said as he strode out of the office.

"Oh man, that isn't funny," Jack groaned.

CHAPTER 6

Kelly sat at the café table waiting for Jennie to arrive. She usually loved lunches with Jennie and if anyone could cheer her up, it would be her. She'd started spying on her boss a few weeks ago and always had something funny or interesting to talk about.

Kelly could never get over how gutsy Jennie was. She was the queen of espionage when it came to getting the scoop on things and probably should have been a journalist. The woman would kill at a career like that.

But she couldn't get in the mood for lunch and gossip today. With no real job prospects in sight, it was beginning to look as if her bachelor's degree in Political Science was every bit as useless as people said bachelor's degrees were nowadays. To top it off, she'd finally received the last of the results of her applications for law school and the news wasn't good.

Well, that wasn't true. Most people would say the news was very good, but if you couldn't pay for your school of choice, it didn't matter if they accepted you.

Kelly looked up to see Jennie coming toward the table and pasted a smile on her face for her friend. She didn't want her bad mood to ruin their lunch, and she didn't want Jennie to feel sorry for her.

"I have juicy gossip today! You won't believe what I overheard," Jennie started off but slowed when she saw the look on Kelly's face. "What's wrong?" Jennie frowned at her friend.

Kelly shook her head and widened her smile. "I'm fine. What juicy gossip?"

Jennie wasn't buying it. She tilted her head and raised her brows in challenge.

"I got my acceptance letter to Yale. I got in," Kelly said.

"What? That's fantastic!"

"I didn't get enough scholarship money to cover even half the tuition there. I thought I had a shot at more grants, but they're getting really tight nowadays. And if I take out that much money in loans, I'll be paying for the rest of my life."

Jennie leaned in and hugged Kelly across the table. "Oh, I'm so sorry. It must feel good to know you got in, though, huh? *Ugh.* That's sounds so 'hey it's an honor just to be nominated,' doesn't it? I'm sorry, Kel."

"I know." She shrugged and tried to smile, but she knew it probably came off somewhat sad.

"How much money do you need?" Jennie asked hesitantly.

"Well, it costs $52,000 per year for three years. I got a few grants and scholarships but only about $18,000 total so when I say I'm short, I mean I'm *really* short. Even if I defer for a year and work the whole time I'm in school, there's no way I'll have enough."

Jennie frowned. "I'm so sorry. I know you had your heart set on Yale, but maybe you can apply to other places? Maybe the state law school?"

Kelly raised her chin. "I will. I'll work for a year while I apply at University of Connecticut for next year and save my money until then. UConn is a really good law school, too. Top fifty."

It was really stupid of her to only apply to one school. She'd told herself some fru fru BS about letting the universe know she was all in so she'd get what she needed. What had she been thinking?

She pasted another bright smile on her face for Jennie. "So distract me. What have your secret spy skills found today?"

In hushed tones, so no one around could hear, Jennie launched into the story of the infamous Jack Sutton's desperate need for a wife.

It was almost ridiculous to think the billionaire couldn't find someone to marry him. He must have women lined up around the block who'd be willing to take a ring to the finger for that man. He was sexy as hell and easily New Haven's most eligible bachelor. In fact, she was pretty sure the local papers had called him that more than once.

From what Kelly knew, he was some genius in the board room, turning companies that were struggling into Fortune 500 companies or something like that. Maybe it was water into gold he was doing. Whatever it was, it was a trick no one else seemed to be able to match to that level.

As Kelly listened to her friend talk, she wished she could sometimes be as brash and brave as Jennie. Really, who had the guts to listen in on their boss's conversations like that?

And from the sound of it, her boss would have to find someone fast to run to the altar with him if he was going to keep his company and get his aunt off his back. In fact, she was surprised Jennie hadn't marched into the room and proposed to Jack right then and there—just for the fun of it.

Propose to Jack Sutton?

Kelly froze. Sure it was a crazy idea, but why not? If she married Jack Sutton for one year, he'd get to keep control of his shares and his job and his company would be secure. She'd get the money to go to Yale for three years. She and Jack would go their separate ways at the end of the year. *Voila!*

Kelly shook herself and tried to get rid of the crazy idea. But the more she thought about it, the more it sounded like a good one. A reasonable idea. The kind of idea she could pull off if she took a page out of Jennie's playbook for once. If she didn't let her doubts hold her back.

"Is Mr. Sutton nice?" Kelly interrupted.

"What?" Jennie asked. "Oh, well, yeah, I guess he's a nice boss. Scares the hell out of most people in the business world. If you cross him or try to cheat him in a deal, look out. I've heard people say he's crushed companies who thought they could pull something over on him. But, he's actually really good to the people that work for him. It surprised me at first. I always thought he would be a real ball breaker."

Jennie leaned forward in a conspiratorial whisper. "He has a whole division that he calls his security division, and they do some cyber security and stuff, but they're really mostly there to investigate any companies he's going to invest in or anyone he's negotiating with. They say he never goes into a deal blind. If you enter a deal with Jack Sutton or walk up to the negotiating table on the other side of him, he'll already know what color underwear you have on that day."

Kelly shifted and looked around. "Well...but I mean, is he a *nice* guy? Like, would you date him or would he be a total jerk to the woman he marries?"

"Noooo, he's not bad," Jennie said slowly, looking at Kelly as if trying to figure out what she was thinking. "He's a really good guy. I guess I'd date him, not that he'd ask me. I mean he dates... Oh my God! What are you thinking?" She pointed a finger at Kelly. "Oh my God! Don't answer that. I know what you're thinking. You're thinking you'll marry him!"

"It could work." Kelly blushed. "I go in there and ask for my tuition in exchange for a year of marriage. We head to the courthouse, then a neat and easy divorce a year from now."

Growing up, she thought she'd marry for love. That when it

happened to her, it would be forever. But she hadn't met anyone who made her think of spending her whole life with them. And a fake marriage would be okay as long as it had an expiration date, and it was to a man she could trust—a good man. It wouldn't stop her from finding the real thing someday, and it meant that she'd be able to get her law degree.

She caught her lower lip between her teeth. She didn't know the man, but Jennie did. And wouldn't she have heard rumors if he beat his girlfriends or something? The man was always in the public eye in New Haven. The press loved him. He couldn't keep anything like that secret for very long.

"Besides," she said as she continued to justify her plan, "I might as well. It's not like I'm going to miss out on falling in love with someone else because I tie myself up with Jack Sutton for a year."

"Kelly, don't be silly. Of course you'll fall in love someday. You just haven't met the right guy yet."

She waved off her friend's words. "Maybe someday, but I've dated some really great guys. I mean really, really great. But I've never felt more than 'like' for any of them—even when they said they were in love with me. I really don't think love is in the cards for me, and even if it is, what are the chances that during the year I take off from dating for a fake marriage, I'll miss out on the *one* guy who I'm destined to fall in love with? I think the chance of that is slim. And, if it's true love that's meant to be, wouldn't it somehow work out after my fake marriage?" Kelly knew how to push Jennie's hopelessly romantic buttons to win the argument.

Jennie stared at her, shaking her head. Kelly could imagine what her friend was thinking.

Jennie was supposed to be the daredevil. Jennie was the one who took risks. She did stupid things. Things with the kind of consequences that could get you in real trouble.

Kelly was the levelheaded, calm, orderly one. The kind of person who most certainly would never do *this*.

Jennie appeared to be speechless as she stared back at her. And if Jennie was speechless, things had to be headed in the wrong direction.

CHAPTER 7

Kelly arrived at Jack Sutton's office a few minutes before three o'clock as she and Jennie had planned. She had run home to print up the marriage license application from the New Haven Office of Vital Statistics website, shower, and dress in black wool slacks and a fitted ivory cashmere sweater.

She left her hair down drying it with a roller brush so it lay in soft waves on her shoulders and went with light makeup she hoped like hell looked classy. Jack Sutton was probably used to classy.

The butterflies in her stomach seemed like they were dancing some sort of coordinated Macarena dance or something. It wasn't pretty.

When Jennie saw Kelly step off the elevator her jaw dropped. "I can't believe you're going through with this. By the time I got back to the office, I was sure you'd chicken out."

Kelly squared her shoulders and stood up to her full height. Not that she was tall at five four, but it made her feel better. "I'm not going to second-guess myself on this. If I keep moving without stopping too long to think about it, I can go through with it, so get me in there."

Jennie raised an eyebrow and Kelly knew she'd owe her friend big time. The scene about to play out would essentially put Jennie's job on the line. By getting Kelly in there, she'd be revealing she had spied on Jack. She had a week left in the temporary placement. With this move, she would most likely lose not only this placement, but any chance of getting a new placement through the temp agency as well.

So yeah, Kelly was going to owe her and then some. But Jennie had told her she was okay with that and Kelly believed her. Jennie got bored staying in one job for too long. She'd bounce back.

"Well, you may be off your rocker, but at least you look good. Jack's Aunt Mabry and his cousin Chad are already in the office. They've only been in there for a minute, though," said Jennie.

"Here goes nothing." She took a deep breath and waited for Jennie to announce her.

With a huge grin on her face, Jennie pushed the intercom button on her phone and calmly spoke into the speaker. "Sir, your fiancée has arrived. Shall I show her in?"

Jack sat in his office with his aunt and cousin and wondered how the hell to explain that there was no fiancée. Andrew had sent a text at two o'clock saying he hadn't found out anything more, but he was working on something. He just didn't say what, so Jack had no idea if he should stall or just come clean.

He had actually been desperate enough to start calling some of the women he'd dated in the last year or so. He wasn't exactly a ruthless player, although the tabloids tried to make it look like he was. Sure, he got around, had a few dates a month and slept with some of them, but those women all seemed shallow and fake to Jack.

Two of them didn't answer the phone, one was gushing about

her new husband and another had moved to London when she was offered a modeling deal with a European agency. That was as far as he got in his little black book before his aunt arrived—twenty minutes early. It seemed Chad had been with Mabry this morning because they arrived together and now they both sat, mother and son, looking expectantly at him.

"We're here to meet Jack's fiancée," a smug-looking Mabry announced to Chad. Jack watched a bemused expression come over his cousin's face.

Chad had to be wondering what the hell was going on. He and Jack were close. They were more like brothers than cousins, so if he were getting married, Chad would have been the first to know.

I'm never gonna' hear the end of this from him.

So there they sat, waiting for an introduction to a fiancée that Jack had never mentioned; a fiancée Chad had never set eyes on.

Jack leaned forward in his chair, took a deep breath and prepared to tell his aunt there was no fiancée.

Or maybe he should see if he could get Chad out of the room first so he didn't have to have this confrontation in front of his cousin.

Just then his secretary's voice cut in, and he could swear he heard her say his fiancée was here.

Jack's experience in business had taught him to school his expressions and hide his thoughts from those around him, and though he wanted to whip around and grab the phone, he didn't. He quickly hid all emotion from his face as he listened to his secretary.

"Sir, did you hear me? Mr. Sutton? Your fiancée has arrived. Shall I show her in?" Jennie spoke again.

Andrew. Andrew must have sent him a fiancée. How in the hell had Andrew found him a fiancée? Really, how does one go about that, Jack thought.

Oh hell. He scrubbed his hand over his face as a possibility hit him. What if Andrew sent him a prostitute?

Jack stood and went to his desk, hitting the button on his phone to engage the intercom. "Uh, yes, send her in, please." Jack forced the words out as his mind raced through the possible scenarios.

Jennie opened the door to his office and stepped aside and a dark-haired woman swept into the room as if she owned the place. She glided over to him, brushed a light kiss on his cheek, and casually handed him a stack of papers.

The soft scent of some kind of flower threw him off his game.

"Hello, sweetheart," the stranger said to Jack before turning to his aunt and Chad. "You must be Jack's Aunt Mabry and his cousin. He's told me so much about you. I'm Kelly Bradley."

She took the hand of a very stunned looking Aunt Mabry and pumped it before she turned to Chad, whose amusement had turned to confused surprise. Kelly shook his hand as well.

"It's nice to meet you," Chad said, but it came out more as a question than a statement. "I don't know where Jack's been hiding you," Chad said with a huge grin on his face.

Jack was too busy trying to figure out who had just walked into his office...and what she was doing, to respond to Chad's dig. This Kelly person had walked in as though she belonged there. As though she and Jack had the kind of intimate, close relationship that lets a woman waltz into a private family meeting and announce herself rather than wait to be invited and introduced.

Whoever she was, she was beautiful. Her hair was a deep chestnut color, and it fell down her back in loose waves over the soft ivory cashmere of her sweater. She had incredible, bright blue eyes and a light complexion with a sprinkling of freckles across her cheeks and nose. Her snug sweater showed off a soft, curvy figure that begged to be held.

Wherever Andrew had found her, he had done well. She was exquisite.

Jack tore his eyes off her and skimmed the papers in his hand while she stood chatting with his aunt and cousin as if nothing were out of the ordinary.

The papers appeared to be an application for a marriage license for the State of Connecticut. There was a yellow sticky note on the top page that said: One year of marriage for $154,000.

He quickly tucked the note in his pocket as his mind flew over possibilities.

Andrew had found him a wife for $154,000.

What the hell?

Had Andrew hired a woman from a call girl service? Asked some girl off the street?

As he did in all of his deals, Jack quickly scanned all potential scenarios in his head. He assessed and evaluated the merits or drawbacks of each. Obviously, if she were a call girl, the drawbacks were significant.

He was woefully uninformed, and that wasn't a position he was used to being in.

What the hell should he do? He had no idea who this woman was, but he didn't have a choice if he wanted to continue to head up the company his father had built. The company Jack had expanded and come to love. Now, he stood stiffly in his office as his head reeled from the sudden proposition in front of him…

Reason kicked in; he had to trust that Andrew wouldn't have sent a hooker or someone he didn't know. Could Andrew have found a willing friend of his? Or maybe an ex-girlfriend? How much would that suck? To marry one of his best friend's exes and pay her to do it on top of that?

Jack hadn't felt so off balance in his life. He suddenly realized that his supposed fiancée was talking to him.

"Jack? Honey, I need to know if you can make it to the courthouse to apply for the marriage license tomorrow? We both have to be there to get it. Does that work for you?" Kelly asked, indicating the papers in his hand.

"Uh, yes. Yeah, that works for me." Jack spit the words out through the haze in his head and turned to smile at his aunt and cousin. No matter what Chad's relationship with Bryan Barton was, it looked as if Jack had just committed himself to a year of marriage with a stranger.

CHAPTER 8

Kelly swallowed hard as she heard Mr. Sutton's answer to her 'proposal.' A tight ball of nerves had been growing in her stomach since she walked in the room, and she felt that tension spreading through her entire being.

Chad excused himself to return to his office with a look on his face that promised his cousin would be grilled for details later. Kelly watched Mr. Sutton out of the corner of her eye as she continued to talk to his aunt.

She had seen Jack Sutton on occasion coming in and out of the building when she'd met Jennie for lunch so she knew he was handsome. But, close up, handsome didn't even begin to describe the man.

Jack was tall, about six feet three inches. He had dark brown hair that curled up at the edge of his collar. His eyes were a rich, deep brown, almost mahogany, and his face had chiseled features with a strong jaw. There wasn't a damn thing about the man that didn't sizzle.

He wore a suit, but even in that Kelly could see his body was hard and fit under it—his tall, lean form toned and strong. His intense gaze made her breath go ragged. She couldn't imagine what it would be like to be alone in the room with him if he had this kind of effect on her with his aunt and cousin with them.

Jack sat on the edge of his desk, legs stretched out and crossed at the ankles in front of him, arms crossed over his chest. He watched her quietly while she finished chatting with his aunt.

Kelly wrapped things up and ushered Mabry out the door by four o'clock as she made excuses about her fiancé needing to get back to work. She closed the door behind his aunt and turned to Mr. Sutton. That's when Kelly felt the ground fall out from under her and her world tilt on its axis.

As she faced Jack Sutton she found herself feeling shaken and uneasy. She looked up at him and realized that, in essence, she had just waltzed into his office and proposed.

"I can't believe I did that." She began to pace frantically. She wrapped her arms around her waist and circled the room.

"Oh God, oh God, oh God." She might hyperventilate. She slid down onto the couch that sat along the longest wall in Jack's office and tried to breathe, but ended up taking in huge gulps of air that felt as if they might choke her.

For the first time since she came up with her harebrained scheme to get her hands on enough money to attend Yale Law School, the reality of what she had done hit her like a ton of bricks. She'd just proposed to one of the country's most eligible bachelors.

And he'd said yes.

CHAPTER 9

*J*ack studied Kelly Bradley as she began to fall apart in his office. She had been so cool and collected two minutes ago—so totally in control of the situation. Now he watched her crumble as if all the steel she seemed to have running through her veins moments ago was suddenly drained, leaving her frightened and panicked.

He smiled wryly and suddenly felt back in control.

I guess it's my turn to be the calm, cool, collected one.

The killer instincts he always felt when he walked into the boardroom or sat down at the negotiating table came back in full force. He crossed to the beautiful woman and took both of her hands in his.

"You did great. You had them completely fooled and you did great. I don't know how Andrew found you on such short notice, but you were fantastic." Jack started to rub her back in slow, soothing circles, hoping to calm her down so they could discuss the details of their newly made arrangement.

"Andrew didn't give me a heads up about this, so you're going to need to calm down and fill me in." He continued to rub her back and he could hear her breathing begin to slow down and become more regular. Jack felt her body relax as her breathing returned to normal. "See," he said, "that wasn't so bad."

Kelly nodded and gave him a weak smile. She took several more deep breaths. Jack watched as her expression moved from panicked to resolved. And then she was grinning, and she was gorgeous.

"Ha! I did it. I knew I could," she said out loud.

Great, she's got multiple personalities or she's bipolar or something. Jack watched as Kelly's emotions swung back and forth.

Then her eyes went round and she sat up straighter. "Wait," she said, "who's Andrew?"

CHAPTER 10

𝒫oker face or not, Jack needed to put some space between them when Kelly asked who Andrew was. Where the hell had this woman come from?

He stood up and took a few steps back and schooled his expression once again. Staying calm despite her revelation that Andrew hadn't set this up wasn't easy but he needed to find out what the hell was going on. If she didn't know who Andrew was, how did she come to be here, and who had he agreed to marry?

What was happening to his ordered world?

"If Andrew didn't send you, then who the hell are you?" Jack demanded. This day was getting worse and worse. Hell, it had to be a nightmare. There was no way he had just agreed to marry some complete stranger in front of his aunt and cousin. A complete stranger who happened to materialize out of thin air right when he needed a wife?

Jack rubbed the heels of his hands against his eyes. He hadn't slept much the night before after he lied to his aunt about having a fiancée, and he was working even more than usual lately. Maybe he imagined this.

That's it. She's a hallucination. A very vivid hallucination.

The hallucination was speaking, though. Do hallucinations speak?

"I'm Kelly Bradley," she said, tentatively.

Jack leveled a steady glare at her and crossed his arms over his chest. "Nice to meet you, Kelly. Now who the hell are you and where did you come from?"

She squirmed under his gaze, just as he'd wanted her to. He wanted the truth and he was damned good at getting it.

"I recently became aware of your problem, Mr. Sutton, and I have my own problem. I put two and two together and figured out we could help each other, and so here I am. Voila," she explained with a little flutter of her hands at the "voila."

"'Jack'" he said, almost absent mindedly. Something in him didn't like her calling him Mr. Sutton. Still, he focused on what she'd said. "'Became aware'? That's a bit vague. Start from the beginning, woman." Jack knew he was a formidable-looking man, and he was using that to his advantage as he grilled Kelly, but he also couldn't help be a little amused by her attempts to skirt his questions.

Damn, she's cute when she squirms.

"Um, well," Kelly bit her lip as she started the story, but he hardly heard her. He found himself distracted by her luscious, kissable mouth.

Jesus, Jack, get a grip on yourself and focus.

Kelly was still talking and he forced himself to listen to what she said.

"Jennie overheard you talking about your mother's will and that you needed someone to marry you by the end of the week. So, here I am. We'll get married for a year and then get a nice neat divorce, and we'll never have to see each other again. I'm not a psycho—just a normal girl with a degree that apparently isn't going to get me a job anytime soon."

She took a breath. "So I improvised. And, before you get all worried, I have zero interest in a real relationship. I have other plans and marriage isn't one of them. And besides, I'm immune to falling in love. I'm broken or something. It just doesn't happen to me, so that won't be a concern." At this point, Kelly was babbling.

Jack held up his finger to stop Kelly's story for a moment. He pushed the button on his phone and spoke. "Jennie, can you come in here, please?" He released the button and turned calmly back to Kelly.

As he faced off with her once again, he asked, "Why $154,000? Why did you ask for such a specific amount?" Gather the information first, Jack told himself. Get the right information so you stay ahead of this thing—whatever the hell this thing was.

"I need it for law school. I got into Yale, but I can't pay for tuition. I need that amount to cover three years so I can get my J.D." she said.

Jack noticed that she raised her chin just a hair as she told him that she had gotten into Yale. As she talked, she began to look more like the confident woman who had claimed his office as her own an hour earlier.

Hmmm. If what she said were true, she wasn't an idiot and—all evidence of mood swings aside—she probably was a fairly bright, normal person to have made it into law school. Much less Yale Law School.

That showed she wasn't completely psychotic, anyway. And she wasn't looking to take him for millions. His rough net worth was a matter of public knowledge, so she had to know the amount she was asking for was chump change to him. She could have demanded millions, and it wouldn't have put a dent in his bank account. He wondered why she hadn't asked for more.

Watching her now, he began to think they just might be able to pull it off. He'd have to teach her about negotiating though. Really, what was she thinking only asking him for tuition? She'd had him over a barrel when she walked in this room. She should have held out for more.

Jack made a mental note to have a full background check done on Kelly. He could have the results back tomorrow. If that panned out, he would go through with getting the marriage certificate the next day as she suggested. If not, he'd send her packing.

While Jack was busy thinking, Jennie came into the room. She looked appropriately embarrassed, trying not to make eye contact with her boss. He figured she was probably wondering if she would get fired from the temp agency or only from this particular assignment.

Jack glanced up at Jennie. "Call the temp agency and tell them you quit. You work for me now. Go down to Human Resources and tell them you're joining Chad's team. Chad runs our security and investigations department. I think that's a good fit for your...*skills*. HR will get you set up."

Jennie stood there with a stunned look on her face, and Jack wondered if she'd ever been caught at any of her little games before.

"Oh, and Jennie," Jack said.

"Yes, sir?"

"Keep the marriage deal quiet. Don't mention it to anyone, including Chad, or you're fired and Kelly won't get a penny. That goes for anything else you've overheard. And tell maintenance to get that damned intercom fixed."

He had known the light didn't work right on the phone but hadn't thought it would be an issue. Hell, usually his company was the one investigating other people. But Jennie had been eavesdropping on him—in his own office. He should have been more careful to protect himself. But at least he could put her to work for him from now on. Jennie had managed to fool him and look so damned innocent this whole time, he was sure she'd be an asset on Chad's team.

As Jennie skittered out of the room, Andrew walked in and looked at Jack and Kelly. "Hey, Jack," he said slowly, "what's going on?" His head whipped back and forth from Jack to Kelly as if he were watching a tennis match.

"Did you find anything?" Jack ignored Andrew's question, asking one of his own. If it was still possible to get out of this marriage deal, he should do it. Even if the woman was stunning and intriguing and gutsy as hell.

"I found a friend of Chad's from prep school that owed me a favor. Says Bryan and Chad knew each other. They weren't close but they also didn't hate each other. Hung out with some of the same people, so it might be a gamble hoping that he wouldn't back Chad for CEO considering his feelings for you. I think we need to go to Chad and get him involved."

Jack shook his head as Andrew finished his explanation. Andrew knew Jack didn't have it in his heart to ask Chad to do that to his mom.

To Jack, family was family and he would lose everything he had, for his family. The irony was, in this case, it was his own family that was attacking him, so he was in a Catch-22. Still, he wanted to do all he could not to hurt his aunt as he defended himself.

CHAPTER 11

Jack faced Kelly again. He was once again fully back in his element. He took control of the negotiations now that he had made the decision to run with this. He didn't really have any other option, and she didn't appear to be a lunatic.

In fact, as he watched her quietly come to grips with what she had done and get her confidence back, he marveled at her. It had really taken guts to walk into the room and pull off what she had. And she'd done it with such grace and confidence. She owned his office as if it were hers, and there weren't many people who could pull that off.

He found himself a little in awe of the gorgeous creature who now sat quietly on his couch.

"One year of marriage. Prenuptial agreement. You get your law school tuition, and you'll have a credit card for expenses while we're married. You'll have to attend occasional dinner parties and fundraising events, that sort of thing, so you'll need appropriate clothes. Some of them will be black tie. You'll put anything you need on my card. After the divorce, I'll get you a condo in New Haven and spending money while you're in school, plus your tuition. After graduation, you'll be on your own. You'll move into my house in Fairfield while we're married. At the end of the year, we cite irreconcilable differences and end the marriage."

"I hadn't really thought I'd need to move in with you. I-I thought this would only be on paper," Kelly stammered while Andrew watched the scene play out, with a look of shock on his face. It was more than obvious Andrew didn't know who this woman was or how Jack had found her.

Jack could see Andrew tensing. His friend had his own reasons to be doubly suspicious when it came to women, but Jack was going with his gut here, and his gut told him this woman wasn't a threat to him.

Jack shook his head. "My Aunt and board of directors will need to be utterly convinced this is a real marriage. We need to live together. There are nine bedrooms so we won't need to sleep together. The house is on the water so you can spend the summer relaxing and hanging out before school. I have a housekeeper who lives in an apartment over the garage, but she's very loyal and discreet. She won't say a word if we aren't sharing a bed."

Kelly blushed at his mention of sharing a bed and Jack found himself intrigued as he watched her cheeks flame red. She was gutsy and courageous one minute and sweet and innocent the next. It was a captivating combination.

Wait.

Jack shook his head to clear his thoughts.

Focus on the big picture, Jack. She's a means to an end. Nothing more.

Andrew piped back in. "I left you alone for three hours and you found a wife?"

"She found me," Jack answered in a distracted manner, not bothering to elaborate.

Andrew raised his eyes to the ceiling and muttered to no one in particular. "Whole industries are built on helping men and women try to find someone, and Jack has women walking in off the street to marry him. Wait, why did she walk in off the street?" Andrew asked as he directed his eyes back to Jack. "She just happened to know you were in the market for a wife? This is like an episode of *I Dream of Jeannie*."

Jack ignored the questions and kept his focus on hammering out the details with Kelly. "We'll have to go out to dinner and things occasionally, maybe kiss once or twice in front of the right people," Jack continued.

Now Jack could really see the heat climbing its way up Kelly's cheeks. He was almost enjoying this and wondered how pink he could make those cheeks burn. Her eyes had gone big and round at the mention of a kiss. What would those doe eyes do if he told her what else he was thinking of doing as he watched her now?

Jack glanced over at Andrew and saw Andrew had one eyebrow raised as he regarded the couple.

He leaned a shoulder on the wall, crossed his arms, and watched the scene unfolding before him. Jack knew he was going to catch a lot of flak about this from Andrew, but he needed to focus on Kelly for now.

Andrew shook his head and muttered something about a bottle and Jeannie and Captain Nelson. Andrew looked amused now, but Jack knew once he heard the full story, he was going to catch hell for what he was planning to do. Andrew didn't have very much faith in women's motives.

CHAPTER 12

Kelly watched Jack as he detailed the terms of their deal. She hadn't really thought through the actual implementation of her plan. Her palms were sweating and her cheeks flamed as she listened and considered the implications. She wasn't a virgin or anything, but she certainly hadn't thought through the possibility they would need to share a bed, so she was relieved to hear she would have a separate room.

She could handle being housemates if necessary, but the thought of kissing Jack made Kelly feel like an inexperienced fifteen-year-old. In a normal world, she wouldn't dream of kissing a man like him.

He was powerful and striking, with a chiseled body and eyes that felt as if they could melt her with a glance. He was also completely out of her league.

When she was with Jack, she felt as if a whole swarm of butterflies had been let loose in her stomach. Her breath came faster and shorter. She felt as if she might pass out when he looked at her with that steady, sensual gaze as if he could look right into her and read her thoughts.

It was impossible not to second guess herself again and again. She shouldn't have done this. She couldn't go through with it.

But based on his words, he was clearly counting on her to marry him in two days. Marry him and move in. She closed her eyes as she felt a tightening in her stomach and wondered for the fiftieth time that hour just what she had gotten herself into.

CHAPTER 13

"Married, my ass," Chad's mother bit out as she walked in his office without knocking. "That engagement is as fake as my highlights. I don't know how he did it or who she is, but we need to expose this marriage as a fraud."

Mabry tossed her purse down on one of the two chairs in front of Chad's desk and lowered herself into the other.

"Hello again, Mom. Long time no see," Chad deadpanned as he turned away from his computer to face his mother.

He didn't know quite what was going on with Jack's sudden marriage announcement, and he agreed something didn't smell right, but Chad would respect his cousin's decision.

He didn't have to tell Jack he was running background checks on her that went so deep she'd probably feel it when they were run.

He had no idea what his mother's angle was and he didn't care. He wasn't going to help her with whatever her latest plot was when it came to hurting Jack. She was on her own with that.

His mother ignored his reply and continued her tirade. "They're going to be married by the end of the week, just in time to meet the terms of his mother's will. There's no way this is a real marriage. I've never even heard him talk about this girl, and all of a sudden they're getting married?"

Ah. So that was it. His mom was going after the stocks in the trust. Chad had forgotten about the terms of Jack's mother's will. Chad had his own shares in the company, though his dad hadn't wanted to invest much early on when the rest of the family got in on it, so most of what Chad owned had come from his own pocket and hard work.

His mother wasn't even pretending to listen to him.

"Nonsense," Mabry said harshly. "We need to put the spotlight on this wedding and end this now before he gets controls of those shares."

Chad waited his mother out. He was used to this from her and if there was one thing he'd learned in the military, it was patience.

He knew he could press her and make her stop, but he'd had trouble putting his foot down with her since his dad walked out on her ten years ago.

That abandonment had changed her. It broke her, and that broke Chad's heart. It was as if she were a different person. She was hard and unreachable sometimes, and other times she was fragile and would have a meltdown at the drop of a hat. She seemed filled with anger.

Chad was afraid if he pushed too hard, and said just plain 'no,' she'd feel as if he were leaving her too.

Mabry ignored the look on her son's face as he continued to sort papers on his desk. "If we can show the board the marriage is a farce, we can convince them Jack isn't fit to run the company even with those extra shares and outvote him. We need to figure out how to prove those two aren't really in love. We need to know who she is and what she's getting out of this."

Chad grit his teeth together. Damnit, it was one thing for him to bitch at her, but he needed to make sure she didn't go too far and hurt Jack. That wasn't something he was willing to let her do.

CHAPTER 14

Jack had never seen Roark turn as red as he was now. If he hadn't been the only person Jack trusted to write the confidentiality agreements and prenup Jack needed, he wouldn't have told the man until after the wedding to Kelly took place.

Jack leaned back in his chair and waited for Roark to finish steaming. He crossed his legs at the ankle and stretched out. They'd be here awhile.

"This was not even remotely what your mother wanted, Jack!"

Jack didn't doubt it, but his mother shouldn't have fucked with his personal life like this.

He felt a flash of guilt at the thought, but it was true. What woman tries to reach out from the grave to manipulate her son into marriage. If he didn't resent that on some level, he wouldn't be normal.

"Roark, you had to know I was going to find a way around this. I'm not losing my company, even if it is to family."

The other man went to the window and looked out over the city. "Don't do this, Jack. You don't even know this woman."

Jack didn't bother to repeat what he'd already told his lawyer several times. The man knew he was having a background check done on Kelly and that she was friends with Jack's secretary.

"She's nothing more than a woman who wants to pay for college. She's not psycho or a gold digger."

Roark turned to him running a hand down his face. "You don't know that."

"You can't argue that I'm not good at reading people. She walked in and asked for only the amount she needed to pay her tuition, Roark. She could have asked for more than that. Hell, she didn't even ask for money towards her expenses or anything. She didn't even round up, for Christ sake!"

His lawyer sank into the seat across from him, shoulders slumped. "Marriage isn't something you buy and sell, son. It's not one of your deals."

Jack had known the conversation would come down to this. Roark had been married to the love of his life for fifty-two years before she died almost a decade ago.

"There's no reason it can't be."

The older man was shaking his head. "What was this company worth when you took over as CEO?"

"You know the answer to that." Jack was beginning to lose patience with the conversation. "A shit ton of millions."

Roark smirked. "Fifty-five million, give or take."

"Your point?"

"You could have sat on that, let it ride, but you didn't."

"No I didn't."

"You've built it up and it's worth close to two billion dollars now. You've hit the billion-dollar mark personally, haven't you?"

"Not seeing the point here, Roark." Jack had Andrew to thank for a lot of that. Jack might be a genius in the boardroom, but Andrew was with money. He'd made Chad, Jack, and Andrew a hell of a lot of money.

"The point is, you should walk away. Build your own

company if you want. Or take a vacation. Expand your volunteer work. Anything. Just don't marry a woman you don't know."

Jack leaned his arms on the desk and rested his head on them. He tried to picture his life without this place. Without his work. He couldn't.

He'd been groomed by his grandfather and father to do this work. This company was everything to his family and everything to him.

"It wouldn't be Sutton Capital, Roark. It wouldn't be the same." He looked up and met the man's eyes. "I'm not giving it up."

Roark's dark eyes were sad as he shook his head.

"Draw up the papers, Roark. Make them airtight. That's the only thing you can do for me right now."

CHAPTER 15

*A*ndrew caught up to Chad that afternoon heading down the hall to the back of the top floor where both of their offices were. Each of them had one of the back-corner offices with Andrew's finance team and Chad's security and tech people spread out around the rest of the floor with them.

Chad shot him a look as Andrew fell in step beside him.

"You're running full background." It wasn't a question. Andrew knew Chad would run full background on Jack's bride. What he wanted to be sure of was that Chad gave him a copy of the results.

And yeah, he wanted to be sure the check was damned thorough. Like knowing what kind of underwear the woman wore kind of thorough.

Chad gestured to his office. "Let's wait until we're alone."

They passed several of Andrew's people and most gave him smiles or nods as he went by.

Chad paused at the door to the office of his righthand woman at the office, Samantha Page. She was a computer genius who Andrew was pretty sure they'd never be able to replace if she ever left.

"Don't forget to eat, Sam," Chad said.

"The wizards have to die," the dark-haired woman muttered as she leaned back in her chair, eyes closed.

"Samantha?" Chad said louder.

Sam shot forward, sitting up in her chair and throwing herself off balance as she overcorrected.

She flushed red and looked at them, brows raised.

"Don't forget to grab lunch." Chad said again before continuing on.

Samantha was brilliant on a computer but she could often get so tied up in whatever she was working on, she would forget things like eating and sleeping.

"Wizards?" Andrew asked.

Chad shrugged his shoulders. "She's designing another multi-player gaming world in her head. She told me once she designs the whole thing in her head before she starts the actual coding."

Andrew didn't have to ask if Chad minded her working on her outside projects while she was at work. Some companies would try to claim ownership of anything their employees created while at the office.

Sutton wouldn't do that, at least not where Sam was concerned. She was one of those employees who got her work done and then some. If she wanted to take a break and let her mind wander to wizards and gummy bears, what did they care?

They reached Chad's office and shut the door after entering.

Chad sat and began tossing pencils at his garbage can, more often than not, getting them in on the first shot. It was one of things he did when his mind was racing. Andrew and the rest of the company had grown to ignore that long ago.

"You're digging deep?" Andrew asked.

Chad nodded. "I was going to check in with you about it. Jack didn't tell me to run a background on Kelly, but seeing as the first I heard of her was when they announced their engagement, I thought it was prudent."

Andrew had to walk a thin line here. He couldn't let on to

Chad about the truth of Jack and Kelly's engagement. But as glad as Andrew was that Jack had a solution to his problem with a woman who, on the face of things didn't seem to be a psycho, he needed to be sure about Kelly before he let his best friend go down this road.

Andrew skimmed that line, hoping to set Chad at ease about Kelly so he didn't go digging into the legitimacy of the wedding, while still convincing him to run the background check he needed to feel right about this himself.

Jack was having someone outside the company run a check for him, but Andrew wasn't one hundred percent sure Jack was thinking clearly on this. His head had been screwed up about this clause in the will and Andrew wasn't convinced he was thinking straight.

"Jack says he met her through Jennie a couple months ago," Chad said. "Did you know they were dating?"

"You interrogated Jennie?" Andrew asked.

Chad shot a scowl his way. "Talked. I don't typically grill the people who work for us."

It wasn't entirely true. There was that time they had a guy in the mailroom stealing from their other employees. Chad had been the one to figure it out and if Andrew remembered right there'd been some grilling alright.

"What did she have to say?" Andrew had been planning to talk to Jennie himself, only she'd been down in human resources filling out the paperwork for her new job.

Chad shook his head. "Said Kelly's just a nice normal person. She and Kelly have known each other for years, met at a yoga class. Kelly's going to law school next year."

Andrew worked to keep his face blank as he nodded. "When will you get her background check?"

"I've already got a basic report. I'll have more by the end of the day."

"You'll share?"

Chad nodded and Andrew stood. When he opened the door, Chad called out to him.

'Hey, you never answered my question."

Andrew turned back. "What's that?"

"Did you know they were dating?"

Andrew could see the hurt in Chad's eyes. The man was trying to hide it, but it was there. And Andrew got it. Jack and Chad were close. It had to have hurt to hear Jack was going to marry a woman Chad had never met, much less even heard of.

Andrew didn't want Chad to think he had known something Chad didn't and make the situation worse.

He shook his head. "No. I didn't meet her before yesterday."

It was the truth. It just wasn't all of the truth.

CHAPTER 16

Two days later, Kelly stood outside the New Haven County Courthouse on Church Street and waited for Mr. Sutton.

She shook her head. *Jack.* If she was going to marry the man, she needed to call him Jack.

She thought about how she would break the news to her mother that she got married without telling her family. Without even introducing them to Jack first.

It would break her mother's heart and her sister wouldn't easily forget the fact that she missed out on being Kelly's maid of honor, but she also knew it was wrong to have her family witness a fake marriage. Asking for forgiveness after the fact instead of inviting them to the ceremony was really her only option.

Kelly tucked her hair behind her ears as she watched Jack striding down the street toward her from his office a block away, and was again taken with how utterly and completely gorgeous the man was.

Just as he took over any room he entered with his presence, he seemed to take over the street as he moved down the sidewalk. Kelly couldn't take her eyes off him as he strode confidently toward her as if he owned the city. People moved out of his way as though he did, too.

Nerves took over as she thought about what they were about to do. It should be a crime to look as good as Jack Sutton. Tanned skin and mahogany eyes that burned through Kelly, and a smile that made her legs turn to mush right there on the sidewalk.

As Kelly stood watching Jack, her palms got sweaty, and for a minute she thought about running—just leaving and forgetting all about this crazy idea. She sighed and, despite her reservations, resigned herself to go through with it. It was her crazy idea to begin with, and she had given her word she'd do it, so she would. It wouldn't be fair to Jack to go back on her word now.

She stepped toward him but her feet had different ideas, tripping over themselves and pitching her forward. Her heart slammed in her chest as the ground came rushing at her and she knew this was going to end badly. She couldn't right herself. Couldn't stop the fall. The concrete was going to hurt.

Then Jack was there, catching her in strong arms that circled her and held her until she had her balance back.

It seemed to take longer than it should have and Kelly had a feeling he was as responsible for the lack of equilibrium as the fall. Her heart was still tapdancing in her chest and she didn't think that was going to stop anytime soon.

Jack smiled at her taking her hands as if he knew she needed to be grounded. Maybe he could spot that she was considering bolting.

He gave her a look that felt as if he could see deep inside her, understood her anxiety, and with it, she felt a wave of calm wash over her. She was ready.

Jack watched the play of emotions that ran across Kelly's face as he walked toward her. There were times when she was so calm and confident, and other times when he could see the panic start to edge onto her face.

He supposed that made sense since it was a bit crazy to walk into his office and propose he pay her for a year of marriage—and then actually go through with marrying a man she didn't know at all. He found it fascinating to watch her shift from one emotion to the next. Hell, who was he kidding? Jack found it fascinating to watch Kelly no matter what she was doing.

Jack thought Andrew was going to keel over in his office that day when he finally wrapped things up with Kelly and explained the situation to his best friend.

Andrew had a protective streak, so although he found her approach mildly amusing, he was more than a little suspicious of her. Jack knew Andrew had damn good reasons for his distrust of women where money was concerned, but even Andrew began to warm to her when Jack explained that she had only asked for law school tuition.

And when the results of the private investigator's report came in the next day with nothing but squeaky-clean results all the way around, he was sold on her. So, it looked as though, for better or worse, he was getting married.

Jack wanted to make this marriage look as real as possible, so he had picked out an engagement ring and wedding bands he thought Kelly might like. As he stood in front of the courthouse with her, Jack took a small box out of his pocket and opened it to reveal an elegant diamond ring in a platinum setting. The diamond was an Asscher-cut diamond surrounded by smaller princess-cut diamonds. Kelly gasped as he placed it on her finger.

"W-what is this for?" she stammered as she stared at the ring.

Jack shrugged a shoulder. "Well, it only makes sense that I would buy you a ring. People will expect it, and I thought this one was pretty. Do you like it?"

It was stupid how much he cared about her opinion. He wanted her to like the ring he'd chosen for her.

"It's beautiful," Kelly said, and she nodded vigorously as she fingered it on her hand. She looked as if she weren't used to the feel of a ring, much less one as heavy as the one on her finger now.

"Good," Jack smiled at her then enfolded her hand in his and they walked side by side into the courthouse. He almost laughed when he realized how much he liked holding hands with Kelly. And in a way, he felt as if he had walked into some bizarre world where nothing he'd known before made sense.

Jack Sutton didn't hold hands. He might put a hand to a woman's back to steer her through a crowd or take her arm to help her from a car. But hold hands? No.

And yet, here he was, happily grabbing her small hand in his large one and trotting up to the altar with her.

They found the right room, signed in and presented the paperwork for their marriage license. The ceremony was short, basic, with two of the courthouse staff serving as witnesses. Kelly now wore a thin platinum band inset with diamonds next to the engagement ring, and Jack wore a thick, plain platinum band on his hand.

When the Justice of the Peace said the final words, "You may now kiss the bride," Jack leaned down and softly, gently, pressed his lips to Kelly's.

The shock of arousal that the small kiss sent coursing through him shocked the hell out of him—and from the look on her face it had done the same to her.

Kelly stared wide-eyed at Jack for a split second before glancing away while he worked to school his expression; covering all emotion that he might have revealed in the split second he'd been caught off guard.

What in the hell was that?

CHAPTER 17

*A*ndrew Weston stepped out of the '66 Corvette that was his newest baby. He'd waited until he found one in the color combo he wanted—silver with red interior—that was in mint condition. Someday he'd do the restoration himself on one of his cars, but that would have to come when he stopped working so many hours.

He jogged, taking the front steps to his grandmother's house two at a time. The door opened and Lydia, his grandmother's housekeeper and cook met him with a wide smile on her face.

Lydia was in her sixties and his grandmother was pushing eighty. The two women were more like mother figures to him than anything else so it wasn't anything out of the ordinary when he wrapped Lydia up in a hug.

"What are you doing here in the middle of the day?" Lydia asked.

"Is that Andrew?" His grandmother called from the sitting room to the right where she and Lydia spent a lot of their time.

"Yep, it's me Nora!"

He didn't call her grandmother like most people did. She'd been Nora to him for as long as he could remember but that didn't mean she wasn't the kind of loving grandmother who spoiled him growing up.

Still spoiled him, as a matter of fact. It made no difference that he was thirty-two.

He got his blond hair from Nora, though her brown eyes hadn't passed through to him. He had his dad's blue eyes, a fact he wished he could erase since looking in the mirror at those eyes every day made him want to break the glass.

"Why are you here?" Lydia asked.

"Is he okay?" Nora called out from the other room, seemingly asking Lydia like she couldn't trust his answer.

"I'm fine," he called back, winking at Lydia as they walked into the sitting room. He wasn't going to mention he was there because his best friend was out marrying a woman he barely knew.

The room was richly appointed with upholstered couches and chairs in matching shades of blues, greens, and pale yellows. The heavy inlaid coffee table and matching end tables should have made the room look stiff and stuffy, but Nora made any space she was in seem welcoming and lived in.

There were small framed photos of Andrew growing up and tchotchkes on every surface of the space. A knitted throw covered Nora's lap and she turned her novel over in her lap to hold her place.

He leaned in and kissed her on the cheek, the feel of her papery thin skin soft against his.

"Am I here in time for lunch?"

Lydia snorted at him. "I should have known you came looking for free food. Just like college."

Andrew turned his best smile her way. Lydia's cooking was easily some of the best he'd ever tasted. He and Jack had come here often in college looking for free food and a place to do their laundry without having to wait for the dorm washers and dryers to be free.

"We've eaten," Nora said.

Andrew's face fell and both women laughed.

"I'll get you something. I have some chicken salad in the fridge and I can warm up some of the leftover pie we had last night."

Andrew groaned. "Please tell me it's apple. I live for your apple pie, woman."

Lydia glowed at his eagerness for her cooking. She always had and he was happy to gush over her cooking any day.

"Apple with walnuts," she said.

Andrew let out a hearty groan of appreciation. When he was a kid, he hadn't appreciated it when she ruined his apple pie by adding nuts to it, but he had to admit, as an adult he loved the addition.

"Perfect. A serving of fruits and nuts. It's doubly good for me. I'm practically a paragon of healthy eating."

Both women shook their heads but they were laughing as he'd hoped they would.

Lydia left the room to fix his food and he lowered himself onto the sofa across from Nora's wing chair. He gave her a quick once over looking for any signs that she might not be well. Her color was good and he could see her ankles since they were propped on a stool in front of her. They weren't overly swollen today, which was always a good sign.

"Now then," Nora said, leveling him with a look. "Tell me why you're really here."

He shook his head, tossing her a grin. "Jack's playing hookie so I'm taking an hour away from the office to visit my two favorite women."

His only favorite women, actually.

"Oh?" Lydia said coming in with a tray she placed in front of Andrew. "Jack's not working today? That's unusual."

She gave a raised brow look to Nora as Andrew dug into his pie, choosing to eat it before the chicken salad sandwich she'd placed on his plate. He'd get to both, for sure, but he saw nothing wrong with starting with his dessert.

"Not the whole day. He's taking a few hours off, that's all."

Nora creased her brow, which in turned creased the rest of her face. "Is everything alright? Jack's not sick, is he?"

Andrew laughed. "We do take time off on occasion."

She waved her hand at him. "Not true."

He shrugged a shoulder and tilted his head at her book. "What's today's novel?"

His grandmother read about a book every day or two in between luncheons and garden parties. Most were mysteries. Sometimes she read romance novels.

He tried not to roll his eyes too much at those.

She held it up and showed him a cover that clearly said it was a mystery. One of those small-town ones that always seemed to involve a cat and a bunch of ladies who were equally adept at knitting and solving crimes. Oh and the town was flush with murders even though it was a tiny town by a picturesque lake somewhere.

But to Andrew, those ones were more realistic than the romance novels where a man and a woman who had nothing in common met and fell in love in the course of a weekend at a resort or a week on the run from a killer.

"Good?" he asked.

"Very. I'm three quarters of the way through and I'm not entirely sure I have the murderer right."

He grinned. "I feel confident in your abilities."

His phone buzzed and he looked down to see a message from Jack.

Done.

Andrew shook his head. Leave it to Jack Sutton to have a single word to say about the fact he'd just married a virtual stranger.

Nora and Lydia looked up as he stood.

"I've got to head back," he said shoving his phone in his back pocket and leaning down to kiss first Nora and then Lydia on the cheek.

As he left, he thought to himself that he really needed to hire more help for the women. His grandmother would fight him on it, but he would feel a hell of a lot better knowing they had someone else in the house to do any heavy lifting and help with chores.

It was an enormous house. There was no way they didn't need more than the weekly cleaning service and yard guy that came biweekly.

CHAPTER 18

Kelly's apartment had been packed up and sublet, her belongings moved over to Jack's house on the water in Fairfield. She and Jack headed there right after the ceremony. She followed his car for the thirty-minute trip, and was relieved to have that time to herself.

When she was around Jack, Kelly felt as though she couldn't breathe. Her whole body tingled when he looked at her, and she was mortified by the thought that he might realize exactly what she was thinking whenever they were together.

She wasn't used to trying to hide what she was thinking and feeling, but it seemed like she shouldn't let him catch on to how insanely over her head she was.

Kelly gasped when they turned into the driveway of what would be her home for the next year.

"Wow," she said to herself as she pulled to a stop. "Just...wow."

'Sprawling' was all that came to mind. His home looked like a beach house on steroids with its cedar siding, rooflines that sloped and met at varying angles, and what Kelly thought might be called gables. She pulled into the circular drive behind his car and laughed. Her little Honda Civic seemed wildly out of place behind Jack's Jag.

"This is it," he said, as he stepped out of his car and looked up toward the house.

Kelly stared at the building. "It's amazing," she all but whispered.

"Come on," said Jack, handing her a key, his warm fingers brushing the palm of her hand. "I'll show you inside."

She looked down at the key. She was amazed how quickly Jack had thought of everything they needed. He had pulled this charade together in a matter of days. Her head hadn't stopped spinning since she walked into his office.

She took a deep breath and vowed to have fun with this. After all, she'd had the guts to walk in his office and pull off this little deal...so why not live up to that new image that had bubbled up to the surface that day?

"I'll need to get you a garage door opener and show you how to work the alarm codes. Mrs. Poole lives in an in-law suite over the garage and takes care of all the cooking and cleaning. You can leave her a list of the food you like and what you want her to stock in the house, and she'll see that it's taken care of," Jack explained as they walked in through the front entry.

"Oh, that's really not necessary," she said hurriedly. "I honestly don't want her to have to do things for me. I mean, I don't want you to have to change things for me. And you don't need to buy my food. Maybe I can just have a shelf in the fridge?"

This really wasn't what she had in mind when she thought up this insane plan. Truth be told, she hadn't even thought it through this far, or thought about what their lives would be like for the next year.

Jack stopped and turned to her, his gaze incredulous. "A shelf in the fridge?"

Kelly cringed. Okay, yeah, so that sounded like they were college roomies or something.

A slow smile split his face and he shook his head. "It's all right, Kelly. Let Mrs. Poole take care of you. She does things for me, so there's no reason not to do them for you, too."

Kelly glanced to the house and then back at him, teeth worrying her bottom lip.

"Come on," he said as he headed up, taking the stairs two at a time on his long, lean legs. "I'll show you the house."

Jack showed Kelly the house and went back to the office to work. Her furniture had been put in storage, but all of her clothes, books, and personal items had been put in the largest of the guest rooms.

Kelly climbed the stairs to her new room and looked out the window to the view of Long Island Sound. She did have to admit, it was stunning here. She was going to be spoiled this year in Jack's fairy tale house.

Walking to the bed with its flowered coverlet and throw pillows, she ran her hand over the blanket and sat. It was plush and luxurious.

Kelly stood to unpack her belongings when a plump woman in her late fifties, with short graying hair that once was brown, and kind smiling eyes appeared in the doorway.

"Oh!" Kelly jumped up. "You startled me."

"I'm sorry." The woman smiled and came into the room. "I'm Mrs. Poole. I saw Jack leave and thought I'd come get you settled in. Did he show you where everything is?" She had a singsong voice that Kelly found soothing and comforting as she immediately started to make herself useful.

Kelly responded to the woman's genuine and warm smile with one of her own. "Thank you, yes. I'm Kelly."

Mrs. Poole opened the curtains and blinds, pulled towels out of the linen closet and brought them into the adjoining bath. She even started to help Kelly unpack.

"Jack showed me around, although I think it will take me a while to get used to it all. With one sister and two brothers, I grew up in a fairly large home, but it was nothing like this."

Mrs. Poole laughed. "It takes a bit of getting used to. You holler if you get lost, and I'll come find you and get you to where you need to go."

The woman whirled around busily, putting clothes away as she chatted about the room. "I've always loved this room. Jack brought in a designer to do everything when he bought the house. I wouldn't have thought of putting yellow with Wedgewood blue, but it turned out beautifully. So light and airy with the white wicker furniture and trim."

"Oh, you don't need to help me unpack," Kelly said, embarrassed to be waited on. "I really don't want to be a burden. I mean... I don't mean... that is I don't ...." Kelly stumbled nervously over the words, not knowing how to explain the situation to Mrs. Poole. She didn't know if Jack had told Mrs. Poole about their arrangement yet or not, but he must have if Mrs. Poole didn't think it was odd that Kelly was staying in a separate room.

Mrs. Poole smiled kindly at her as she crossed to hang several dresses in the walk-in closet. "It's all right, dear. Jack explained what's going on. He thought it would be best for me to know about the arrangement. I have to say, it's one of the funnier pickles he's gotten himself into, and I do find it entertaining that the whole thing was your idea. I'll bet *that* caught him off guard. Jack is used to being in charge of things. I bet he damn near jumped out of his skin when his 'fiancée' walked into his office." She laughed a full belly laugh as her eyes sparkled with amusement.

Kelly let out her breath and smiled at Mrs. Poole. The older woman's blunt manner put her at ease, and she had a feeling she would like getting to know this woman.

"Besides, it'll be nice to have someone else around this big place. All of my kids are long grown, and it's too empty here when it's just me and Jack. I like having people around the house to spoil."

Kelly started to relax and felt better about the whole bizarre situation.

But Mrs. Poole's next comment caught her off guard again, and she realized she'd need to stay on her toes.

"That man needs this, though. You'll be very good for Jack, even if it is only for a year," Mrs. Poole said with a wink and walked out of the room.

CHAPTER 19

Jack and Kelly drove to Hamden for her parents' weekly Sunday dinner. They were in his Jaguar, and she couldn't help but appreciate the buttery softness of the leather as she melted down into the seat. It was nothing like her little civic.

"Are you close to your family, Kelly?" Jack asked as he turned off the highway at the sign for Hamden.

"I am. I don't make it for dinner every Sunday, but I try to get there two or three times a month. My mom is a great cook so it's not a hardship," she said, with a small smile.

Jack made a left turn onto a tree-lined residential street. "Tell me again how many of you there are?" She had told Jack about her brothers and sisters before, and she suspected that in his line of work, he remembered names and details with very little effort. Kelly had a feeling he wanted to keep her talking to calm her nerves and she was thankful to him.

"There are four of us. My sister Jessica who's two years older than I am, and our older brothers Liam and David. My sister and my mom and I are really close, so I know they'll be hurt I didn't tell them about you." Kelly chewed on her bottom lip and looked out the window as he pulled over to the side of the street in front of the house where she grew up.

"You ready?" Jack asked her when she made no move to open the car door.

"Better get it over with, huh?" she said, but she looked far from convinced of that idea as she stepped out.

Jack ran around to meet her, and took her hand in his as they stepped along the walkway. Kelly was surprised by how supportive and nice he was about meeting her family. She hadn't expected this big business mogul to be so accommodating. So genuine and sweet. But he kept proving her wrong.

"It'll be all right, Kel." He squeezed her hand, and for a moment Kelly felt as though they had been friends forever with the easy way he had fallen into calling her 'Kel' and the way he was able to calm her whenever she began to feel as if she had fallen down a rabbit hole—which was a lot lately.

She opened the front door and pulled Jack in behind her, still holding his hand. "Mom, Dad," Kelly called out, "we're here."

Kelly's mother came walking in from the kitchen wiping her hands on a dishtowel. "Who's here, Kelly? Did you bring a friend?" Her mom stopped when she saw Jack. "Oh, you brought a friend," she said, all smiles and beaming. Kelly knew her mother was thrilled that she had brought home a man. Just wait until she found out he was a married man. *Her* married man! How would she react then?

"Jim!" her mother called out over her shoulder. "Come meet Kelly's friend."

"Mom, this is Jack. Jack, my mom, Betty Bradley."

Just then her mom spotted the diamonds on her left hand and gasped. Taking Kelly's hand in hers she stared, gaping. Watching the pained look on her face, Kelly tried to get out the words.

"Um, Mom. Jack and I.... We, um...." Kelly couldn't figure out the right way to tell her mother she had missed her daughter's wedding.

"Ma'am...." Jack put his arm around Kelly. "Your daughter gave me the honor of becoming my wife," he said in a somewhat old-fashioned way that was probably very out of character for him, but was absolutely the perfect way to explain things to her mom. Kelly felt a surge of gratitude for Jack and sank further into the curve of his body.

Kelly watched as her mother absorbed the news, but the shock on her mother's face was all she could see. She didn't know if her mother was happy or mad or what.

"Jim!" Her mother really bellowed now. "Come meet Kelly's new husband." Her mother's voice raised in pitch with each word so that she was practically squeaking at the end.

Kelly felt nervous laughter bubbling up as the front hall was quickly filled with her father's large frame, her two older brothers, who both stood as tall as Jack and were both glowering at him, and her older sister—all talking at once.

Jack kept his arm around her, and Kelly grabbed onto his hand as it wrapped around her waist, clinging to him as if he were an anchor.

Her anchor. She didn't know what to say. Jack's calm voice broke through the madness once again.

"Sir," he said, extending his hand to shake hands with Kelly's father, "I'm sorry we didn't come to see you all first. It's just that this took us a bit by surprise."

Kelly almost laughed at Jack's explanation, but she also knew that he was trying to throw himself under the bus for her, and she was in awe that he would go to these lengths to take the fall with her father.

She knew not many people could ever say they'd heard such a humble apology coming from Jack Sutton. The look on her father's face was priceless, and her brothers even seemed to relax slightly as they watched her father take Jack's hand and shake it.

Suddenly, her mom and her sister were pulling her into the kitchen as her sister squealed with excitement and looked at the diamond on Kelly's hand. Jack was dragged off by her brothers and father to the study for a drink. She could only hope he would survive until she managed to rescue him.

Jessica held Kelly's hand tightly and gaped at the ring on her finger, but all Kelly could do was look at her mother's face. There was no anger, just pain. She could see her mother was trying to hide the pain and it tore Kelly up. She had known this would be hard, but she almost wished her mother would yell and scream. Anything would be better than this silent look of hurt.

"I'm sorry, Mom," Kelly said quietly. "I know you probably wanted to be there, but we just had a private ceremony at the courthouse. It was all so fast ...." She broke off, not sure what more she could say to try to explain something that really couldn't be explained.

"Are you pregnant?" Jessica asked in her melodramatic stage whisper.

"Oh, Jessica, don't be ridiculous," Kelly's mother swatted at Jessica and turned to look at Kelly for a good long moment.

In her quiet way, her mother asked her, "Are you happy, Kelly?"

Kelly nodded, "Yes, Mom, I really am." *Not for the reasons you think, but yes, I'm happy.*

Her mother gave one swift bob of the head. "Then I'm happy, sweetheart. That's all I needed to hear." And with that, Kelly was wrapped in her mother's arms. She couldn't shake the feeling of guilt, though, and somehow her mother's quick forgiveness made it worse.

CHAPTER 20

Kelly was sitting next to Jack at the dinner table, but he couldn't read her face as they passed around bowls and platters; filling plates with her mom's homemade chicken, macaroni and cheese, salad, and green beans. It was comfort food at its finest, and he wouldn't mind coming to more Sunday dinners if her mom's cooking tasted as good as it looked.

"So, Kelly, Jack tells us you met at his office?" Her father's question sent Kelly's iced tea down the wrong pipe so that she coughed and sputtered. Jack laughed and patted her on the back while she tried to catch her breath.

"Um, yes, Dad. We met at Jack's office," she finally managed to spit out.

"Oh, what do you do, Jack?" asked her mother.

"I'm in venture capital. My company identifies companies at various stages of development that we think are good risks to invest in. Sometimes they need seed money, sometimes growth or expansion. We invest, and we get a share of the company if they're a success."

When Kelly's mom smiled warmly at him and said, "That's

nice, dear," in a way that Jack knew would sound condescending from some people, he realized she meant it quite sincerely.

She almost said it as if she were proud of him, and he found himself missing his own mother. Searching for another topic of conversation, Jack turned to Kelly.

"Did you tell your parents about Yale, Kel?" Jack had been referring to the fact that Kelly now had a way to pay for Yale, but he was surprised to discover she hadn't even told them yet that she had been accepted. The room went silent as everyone looked at Kelly.

"Oh, no, I haven't told them. I mean, we've had the wedding and everything. Then moving, you know," she said a bit weakly.

"Kelly got into Yale Law School!" Jack surprised himself with how much pride he felt as he announced her big news. He found himself taking a hold of her hand on top of the table.

Once again, the family all talked at once as they congratulated Kelly and talked over each other in their excitement. When things quieted down, though, Kelly's mom spoke up softly.

"Kelly, dear, how much is that going to cost? I'm not sure we'll have the money for Yale. Did you apply to any other schools, sweetheart?"

Now Kelly, Jack, and Jessica, were all sputtering in their drinks and trying to recover, while the rest of the family looked on with confused looks on their faces. Jessica recovered first and grinned at everyone.

"You need to start reading the paper, Mom. Everyone knows who Jack Sutton is. Kelly's rich now. I mean disgustingly rich. As in, filthy stinking rich with a capital R," she said with very little tact or grace, and Jack laughed as Kelly's face turned red.

An hour later Jack stepped out the back door of Kelly's parents' house and walked across the lawn to the oak tree where his new wife stood. Sticking his hands in his pockets and rocking back on his heels, he stood behind her and followed her gaze out to the sunset that created purple clouds spreading across the sky.

"Beautiful, huh?" Kelly asked, looking over her shoulder at him.

"Incredible," he said quietly, looking at her instead of the sunset. Kelly looked down at her toes and blushed.

"I'm so sorry, Jack," she said as she looked up at him. She bit her lower lip.

His eyebrows shot up on his forehead. "For what?" Jack asked, genuinely confused.

"For the mortifying dinner conversation. One minute my mom is practically telling you what a 'nice little company' you have, and the next my sister is announcing your net worth."

Kelly cringed, and Jack imagined she was playing back her interpretation of the night's events in her head.

He laughed a genuine, full laugh which wasn't something that happened often. "I'm very used to people talking about my money. And I happen to like your mom. She makes me think of my own mother and I like that, Kel."

She craned her neck and looked back at him, and he hoped she saw he meant what he said.

Her blue eyes sparkled as she watched him and he caught the scent of flowers again. He stepped in closer to her. He wanted to lean in and breathe her in, soak up the scent of her. He wanted to touch and taste.

"I've been thinking, though, Kelly," Jack went on, as he took her shoulders in his hands and leaned in to speak close to her ear, his breath whispering over her neck, the sweet scent of her doing wicked things to him. "If a newly married man comes to dinner at his wife's house, and they sneak off into the yard together for a private moment...."

He turned Kelly to face him and pulled her into his arms, wrapping her up. He liked the way she felt there. "They would steal a kiss."

He paused and looked into her as he watched her quiet gasp of understanding. A slow smile worked its way across his face.

Jack wanted it to look like they were really married, but he also had to admit he'd been wondering what it would be like to kiss Kelly, to really kiss Kelly, especially after that small kiss at their wedding a few days ago.

And, he was used to getting what he wanted.

He leaned down and brushed his lips softly along her neck before drawing back and looking her in the eye. "I'm going to kiss you now, Kelly," he said, nothing more than a murmur.

He closed his mouth over hers, exploring her slowly, tenderly.

Jack didn't mean to get carried away. Just a little show to make things look the way they should to the world around them.

Somehow that small kiss exploded between them, and he found himself deepening the kiss, pulling Kelly even tighter to him as he delved into her mouth.

He felt her hands come up to his chest and for a moment he thought she would press him away, but instead her small fists closed tightly, grabbing his shirt and pulling him even closer as she came up on her toes.

Heat erupted between them and he was lost. His entire body responded to this woman, going tight and hard in an instant.

Kelly had been forced to focus on keeping her voice steady and her hands from shaking while Jack stood behind her watching the sunset. With him standing so close, it felt as if her body were reaching out to him, or maybe it was his body reaching out to set hers on fire.

She felt the heat of him and knew if she leaned back she would feel hard planes and muscles, but at the same time, he'd be warm and soft and welcoming. She felt herself go damp at just the thought of being pressed against him, her back to his chest. She knew if she did, she'd feel the hard length of him pressing into her and that made her chest tighten at the thought of it.

When he turned her and kissed her, Kelly felt her world suddenly spin sideways, out of control. His kiss was filled with burning passion, and she felt a tingling sensation zip through her body as she fisted Jack's shirt in her hands, pulling him tighter to her.

The second she realized what she'd done, Kelly gasped and let go of his shirt, pulling back from the kiss—but it was too late. She felt the strength of the attraction, the odd pull toward Jack.

He held her close, molding her body to his. Heat spread through her and she knew she had never felt a kiss like that before, and was fairly sure she never would again. And that thought terrified her because this was temporary. This wasn't real. And she didn't fall in love with men. She just didn't.... *Did she?*

Jack looked as stunned as she felt, his deep brown eyes seeming to go even darker with pleasure as he looked at her.

He licked his lips and looked as though he might say something. Or kiss her again and God, yes, please that would work for her.

Before either could say or do anything more, the back door swung open and her brother was there.

"Stop pawing my sister and come in for dessert, mom says."

"There's a dessert joke in there somewhere," Jack said, taking her hand and pulling her toward the house as her head spun and her heart stuttered in her chest.

CHAPTER 21

Jack was surprised to find he liked being married to Kelly more than he thought he would. She finished her registration for Yale and he sent the tuition in as promised, so she was all set to start school in September. Now they had the entire summer to spend figuring out what their lives would be like for the next year.

Over the next week, Jack, Kelly, and Mrs. Poole fell into a comfortable routine around the house. Jack left for work before Kelly got up in the morning so they didn't see each other before work, but he started coming home for dinner in the evenings.

It was amazing how much he looked forward to the time he spent with Kelly at night; liked talking to her and having someone at home to be with at the end of the day.

Mrs. Poole often sat down and ate with them, instead of leaving a plate warming in the oven for him as she had before Kelly arrived. When Mrs. Poole headed back to her room, he and Kelly went into the den to watch a movie or TV together. After a movie, he would go into his office to work, and Kelly would read a book before heading up to her room.

After a week of falling comfortably into their newfound life together, Kelly got up earlier than usual and entered the kitchen as he stood behind the center island, eating yogurt and waiting for his coffee to brew.

He was still wearing his running shorts and T-shirt from his morning run, and he was sweaty and rumpled.

Still, he smiled at the unexpected sight of her. "Morning, Kel. What are you doing up so early?"

She took an orange from the refrigerator and started to peel it, holding the garbage can open with one foot as she tossed the peels. When she was finished, she climbed onto one of the bar stools at the kitchen island. "I'm going job hunting today. I want to see if I can find something other than temp work before school starts."

Jack's smile turned to a frown. "Kelly, I really will pay all of your expenses during law school. I'll even give you spending money. You're going to be working hard enough at school as it is. You should relax for the summer and then focus on studying when you start school. I'll take care of everything else."

He couldn't believe Kelly wanted to work when she was being handed a free ride. She really had no idea the magnitude of the favor she was doing him by giving up a year of her life to save his ass.

And it wasn't the first time Jack realized she was nothing like the women he knew and dated in the past. Hell, they would have taken what he offered and started running up tabs for clothes, jewelry and trips to the spa.... Instead, here she was getting up early to look for work.

She shrugged noncommittally. "I don't really want to take advantage, Jack. We had a deal for law school, but you don't need to do more than we bargained."

"Kelly," he said and tried to figure out if she was for real. "You're doing me a huge favor with this deal. I don't mind making sure you don't have to work while you're in school. I mean it. Let me do this for you."

Jack knew how to read people and right now she looked as if

she was scrambling for some way to change the subject. She glanced down at his leg at the small Celtic sun tattoo on his left calf. "You have a tattoo?" Kelly said with a distinct tone of surprise in her voice.

Jack laughed as he let her switch topics, at least for the time being. "Yup. A bunch of us got them together our senior year." He didn't tell her he was drunk.

"What about you?" Jack continued. "Any hidden tattoos I should know about? I mean, in case someone quizzes me on 'all things Kelly.'"

His grin faded and his mouth fell open when she casually hopped down off her bar stool and tugged the edge of her sweatpants down to reveal a tiny daisy over her right hip bone. It was no more than the size of a quarter, and the strip of skin she was showing was only two inches wide, but Jack was suddenly very grateful he was standing behind the island.

Her skin was creamy and soft and his hands itched to reach out and slide over the spot before dipping lower, exploring what was under the loose sweatpants.

He knew from that kiss the other day that her mouth would taste sweet and she'd melt into him if he put his hands on her again.

He stepped in closer to hide the effect her little reveal was having on him, and managed to choke out some kind of response before she went outside to grab the newspaper for her job search.

Jack watched Kelly leave the kitchen and realized he couldn't live with this woman for a year and treat her like a housemate.

He wanted her, and he usually got what he wanted.

Where Kelly was concerned, he decided to make damn sure he did. He would convince her that their temporary marriage should include all the benefits of marriage while it lasted.

CHAPTER 22

After she grabbed the newspaper from the driveway, Kelly went inside and climbed the stairs to her room. She was relieved she and Jack coexisted as housemates more than as husband and wife since she wasn't looking for anything further. She only wished she would stop fantasizing about the man every time she saw him—and, for that matter, when he wasn't around.

She tried to ignore her physical reaction to him and figured it would go away eventually, but for now, the attraction was powerful and it wasn't easy to put aside.

When she found Jack in his running clothes in the kitchen, hair damp and sweaty from his morning run and those curls of hair edging their way to his collar, it was a lot more than she could handle.

His T-shirt looked soft and comfortable as if it had been washed hundreds of times, and had well-worn, threadbare, see-through spots that gave more than a hint of the muscles underneath it. It had still been slightly damp from his workout so it clung to his abs, showing off the cut of each muscle on his stomach.

She felt like an idiot the second she pulled down the waistband of her sweats to show him her tattoo. He probably thought she was trying to throw herself at him in some lame attempt to flirt.

Kelly wasn't an idiot. She knew Jack dated supermodels and had even dated a famous actress a few years earlier. Although she was confident about her looks and knew she was attractive, she wasn't *that* attractive.

She saw herself as girl-next-door kind of cute—appealing in a sweet way, not in a hot, sexy, leggy-blonde-model sort of way, so Jack wouldn't be interested in her. Besides, she reminded herself again, she didn't want a relationship. The whole point of this marriage was for her to be able to go to school and get her degree, not to hop into bed with the man.

So, yeah, she needed to try to hide her reaction to him. The last thing she wanted to do was let him see that she was panting for him whenever she was near him. Or that he'd begun to star in some pretty x-rated dreams at night. Thank God they weren't sharing a bed.

How mortifying would it be to wake up and find herself dry humping her husband in her sleep.

She groaned. This was bad.

Kelly opened the newspaper and spread it across her bed. Maybe she should get a job she could work at night so she was out of the house when he was home.

She could waitress. That could get her out of the house right at dinnertime.

Too bad she didn't want to give up her time with him at night.

She scanned through the paper and spotted an ad for a legal clinic.

That might not get her out of the house at night, but it would be a great place to volunteer if she wanted to get some experience in working with legal issues.

And if Jack was really serious and he didn't mind paying for her expenses, maybe she should take him up on it and volunteer at the clinic instead of getting a job.

She stood and left her room, planning to make another cup of tea when she heard the front door shut. She went to the hallway window just in time to see Jack getting into his car. He looked up and caught her watching him.

Because, of course he did.

She felt the heat rush to her cheeks but she didn't duck out of sight. She raised a hand and waved goodbye.

He winked at her and grinned.

Of course.

CHAPTER 23

The following Monday, Jack sat in his office getting ready for a meeting when his Aunt Mabry showed up unannounced. His secretary showed her in, and Jack forced a smile to his face as he greeted her.

"To what do I owe the pleasure, Aunt Mabry?" There was a time when Jack would have said those words and meant them. He used to love his Aunt Mabry, but something changed her over recent years and he couldn't connect with her anymore. She had become obsessed with seeing her only son, Chad, as CEO of the company.

He knew the intent was to hurt him, but he and Chad agreed long ago not to let her come between them. He'd play her games because she was Chad's mother.

"Jack, darling..." She breezed into the room. "I've decided to redo my kitchen and the downstairs floor of my townhouse. Chad has a friend staying with him right now, so I need to stay at your place for a few weeks until my kitchen is completed."

He had to work to keep from rolling his eyes. He knew perfectly well what she was doing. She wanted to spy on him and Kelly. There was no way she'd be redoing her kitchen if she didn't want an excuse to stay with him.

And she would normally stay at the Omni downtown or at a spa by the water instead of with him. She had never stayed at his house before, not for a day in his life, even when his mother was alive.

His mind filtered through the excuses he could give her, but when he quickly weighed all of the factors, he decided it was best to let her move in for a bit to get her off their backs.

Besides, if his aunt were around, they'd have to pretend to be husband and wife a lot more often, and he liked pretending where Kelly was concerned. He had to hold back the grin that threatened to show at the thought.

With unexpected enthusiasm, he turned to his aunt. "Sure thing, Aunt Mabry. You're welcome anytime. When do you need to move in?"

"Right now," she said with a Cheshire cat grin of her own. "I'll head over there right now."

With that announcement, she sailed out of the office as breezily as she had waltzed in. Jack stared after her for a minute before reality dawned on him. He and Kelly didn't share a room.

Oh, hell. His aunt wouldn't buy the happily-ever-after marriage if she found out they had separate rooms. He grabbed the phone to try to catch Kelly or Mrs. Poole in time to warn them.

Kelly whipped through the house and up the stairs, calling out as she ran. "Mrs. Poole! We have to move! We have to move!"

Kelly continued yelling as she ran into her room and grabbed drawers full of clothes and piles of hangers with slacks and dresses on them.

Half of the items fell from the hangers and Kelly cursed as she scrambled to pick them up.

Mrs. Poole came up the stairs with a puzzled look on her face.

"What on earth are you hollering about?" she said as she tried to enter the room.

She had to jump out of the way as Kelly made a mad dash to the master bedroom.

"We have to move all of my stuff into Jack's room. His Aunt Mabry is on her way here, and she's staying with us for a couple of weeks," Kelly blurted out as she ran back down the hall to gather more of her belongings.

"Oh Lord," Mrs. Poole rolled her eyes and followed after her.

She grabbed up clothes and toiletries and rushed down the hall to Jack's room. They repeated the trip half a dozen more times as they transferred everything and set it into place. Mrs. Poole cleared out half of Jack's dresser and closet and made room for Kelly's things, while Kelly folded and put her clothing away.

She draped a few things over the chaise in the corner of his room to make it appear as though the two had been living in holy matrimony since day one.

Kelly pulled open the top drawer of the bureau and saw Jack's boxer briefs folder neatly on one side. She shoved her period panties—the ones that were soft cotton and loose and so far from sexy she could cry—to the back of the drawer. She stacked the few matching lacy sets of panties and bras toward the front.

She never dreamed Jack would be looking at her underwear when she started this.

She looked around the room. Maybe she should just put her underwear in a box in the closet or something so he wouldn't see it.

"I'll run these things up to the attic," Mrs. Poole said, grabbing the heavy clothing she'd taken from the back of Jack's closet to make room.

Kelly nodded and started shoving the rest of Jack's things under the bed. He would probably cringe to see her treating his cashmere sweaters like that, but that's what he got for not putting his fall clothing away when the weather turned warmer. The man had a ridiculous amount of clothing.

Kelly put away the last of her things and took a deep breath as she turned to survey the masculine-looking room.

There was a dark mahogany dresser and matching armoire against the deep green walls. Large windows looked out on the same beautiful waterfront view that her guest room windows had shared. The green lawn stretched past the pool, down to a stone wall. Past the wall was the beach and ocean, a scene she would never get tired of.

She turned back to the room and held her breath when her eyes landed on the king-sized bed in the center.

Until that moment, she'd been too panicked about moving to think this through. It hadn't occurred to her that she and Jack would now have to share a bed.

Kelly's smile fell away as she realized that keeping her attraction hidden from her husband just became a lot more difficult.

CHAPTER 24

Kelly stood with Mrs. Poole and Mabry in the kitchen when Jack came in from work that evening. She had poured a glass of wine for herself and Mabry and turned to ask Mrs. Poole if she wanted one.

Out of the corner of her eye, she saw Mabry's eyebrows shoot up but chose to ignore the look. Apparently, in her world, Mrs. Poole was paid help, and one didn't ask the help if they want a glass of wine.

Wait until she sees Mrs. Poole sit down to dinner with us.

Kelly smiled.

Jack walked into the room and said hello to Mrs. Poole and planted a peck on Mabry's cheek before turning to take Kelly into his arms.

She stiffened in his arms. This wasn't part of their nighttime routine.

"Hello, beautiful," he said before he ducked his head to kiss her. It was a warm, gentle kiss, but she could feel the arousal bubbling just under the surface, and knew that if either one of them moved to deepen the kiss, the passion would rise to the surface quickly.

Her body didn't seem to understand how problematic this

could be. It melted into him without her say so and her arms came up around his shoulders.

Damn, I'm going to make a fool of myself if he keeps kissing me like this!

As Mrs. Poole set dinner out on the table in the dining room, Jack asked his aunt how she was settling in and made small talk about things at the office. But Kelly's attention was only half on the conversation. Her mind and her eyes kept wandering to Jack and the strong cut of his jaw, the short growth of stubble that had grown over the course of the day. She didn't think she would ever get tired of watching that man.

She raised her fingers to touch her lips where his had been a moment before, and marveled that she could still feel them burning in response to his touch. When Jack was near, her whole body seemed to vibrate as if pulled by some invisible force.

Drawn out of her thoughts as they sat down to eat, Kelly caught the raised eyebrow on Aunt Mabry's face when Mrs. Poole joined them.

She didn't care. She wasn't used to being waited on and she enjoyed Mrs. Poole's company, so she planned to make sure Mabry didn't have a chance to change the way things happened around the house.

She turned to Mrs. Poole and included her in the conversation. The two were chatting about new recipes to try when Mabry cut in.

"I was thinking we should host a party to celebrate your marriage. The reception you never got to have since things were so—" Mabry paused for effect, "rushed. Something out on the lawn by the water would be lovely. A summer cocktail party, perhaps?"

"That's a great idea," Jack said, surprising Kelly. "How about three weeks from now? Is that enough time to plan things, Mrs. Poole?"

Jack didn't know why Mabry made the suggestion or what she

had up her sleeve, but he figured that the more they went along with Mabry, the faster they'd convince her to back off and leave them alone.

"Sure," Mrs. Poole said. "We'll need to get invitations out right away, but if Kelly can work on that, I can coordinate with caterers and take care of renting tents and lighting. An early evening party would be lovely, with tents and lights all over the lawn as the evening comes on. Kelly and I can do a tasting with the caterers this week and decide on a menu." Mrs. Poole quickly rattled off details while Jack turned to Kelly.

"This will give you an excuse to go shopping. You'll need a cocktail dress. You have my card?" He turned to his aunt and continued.

"Aunt Mabry, maybe you can take Kelly into New York this week and help her find a dress?"

Kelly nodded woodenly. What had just happened? When had everything in her world spun so far out of control.

After dinner, Mabry joined them when they decided to watch a movie. Jack pulled Kelly down next to him and wrapped his arms around her waist snuggling her into him. She tensed for a moment, but as the movie began, he felt her relax and she eventually even rested her head back on his shoulders.

He was struck by the irony of his fake life with Kelly. No woman had ever come close to inspiring the kind of feelings in Jack that his father and mother had shared. With Kelly, he found he really liked his fake life with her and wanted more of it. It was just his luck that the first time he was feeling anything more than base sexual attraction was with a woman he was paying to be his temporary wife.

Jack had known it would feel good to have her in his arms, but he had no idea how good. He was actually glad to have his aunt in the house; to have an excuse to wrap himself around Kelly, to kiss her and touch her as he would if she were really his wife. The smell of her shampoo was enticing; a mixture of jasmine and something else he couldn't identify. It made him think of summer nights, and he found himself wanting to bury his head in the scent of her and nuzzle her neck. With her curvy figure fitting perfectly against him, he had difficulty focusing on the movie. Instead, Jack's mind was assaulted with images of her in his bed, entwined in his arms, under him, over him, looking down from on top of him with her beautiful curly waves of hair framing her face above him. He felt as if he were under attack, and he seemed to be defenseless against this woman.

Jack could feel Kelly's breathing speed up, and knew she was feeling the same things he was. He stifled a laugh when she hopped off the couch half an hour into the movie and yawned.

"I'm more tired than I thought I was. I think I'll head up to bed early. Good night, Aunt Mabry. Good night, Jack," she said as she all but ran from the room.

"Good night, sweetheart," Jack barely managed to get out before she was gone.

~

Kelly sprinted up the stairs and tried to clear her head of the images of her and Jack together, wrapped around each other on the couch, but when she slid in between the sheets after getting ready for bed, she groaned. She had forgotten she would be getting into Jack's bed, and she was once again surrounded by his scent.

As she sank into Jack's arms while they watched the movie, she fought to remind herself that this wasn't real; that he was only putting on a show for his aunt. The hard part was dealing with how incredibly aroused she was as she leaned against Jack's hard chest. She smelled his aftershave, a slightly spicy but clean smell that wasn't overpowering. Her brain began to feel like scrambled eggs when he absentmindedly rubbed his thumb in small circles on her arm. She began to wonder what his hands would feel like on the rest of her body—what those small circles would do if applied to the right place. Kelly had a feeling Jack would know just where to touch her, just how to touch her, to make her melt. If she didn't do something about this soon, she'd be crawling all over him.

She had fought to focus on the movie and ignore his scent, his presence, the hard feel of his strong body underneath her. But no matter how much she tried, she couldn't stop the flood of arousal between her legs, the tingling need in her breasts as she ached to feel his hands on her without her clothes on, and without someone else in the room. In the end, Kelly had to flee the room or risk letting him know what a fool she was, how attracted to him she was. She didn't want Jack to know that she didn't have it in her to fake it around his aunt, or that she was falling for real and didn't know how much longer she could control herself.

CHAPTER 25

The morning after her first night in Jack's bed, Kelly woke to find he had already left the room. She heard him come in the night before and held her breath as she listened to him get ready for bed. She feigned sleep as he brushed his teeth and slipped out of his clothes.

When he slipped between the sheets in nothing but boxer shorts, she thought she would burst, but she focused on keeping her breath steady so she wouldn't have to face Jack.

With a sigh, Kelly slipped from the bed, showered. dressed, and headed downstairs for breakfast. She found Jack, Mabry, and Mrs. Poole in the kitchen.

"Good morning, dear," Mrs. Poole called out cheerfully, making Kelly smile. Jack and Mabry looked up, and she wished for a moment that the smile that came to Jack's face as he looked at her was genuine and not for Mabry's sake.

"Good morning, sweetheart," he said as Kelly joined them at the breakfast nook with her coffee.

"Morning," she smiled shyly at Jack across the table. Kelly smiled and nodded at Mrs. Poole as she put a plate of eggs and toast in front of her.

Kelly's eyes dropped to the stack of newspapers Jack read

every morning. There was one from their local area, two from New York, and several European papers.

One of the New York newspapers sat on the table, the words "No Ransom Calls, Families Hopeless" above a string of photos showing five smiling and seemingly carefree women. She pulled the paper closer to read the article.

"I thought we might have lunch today," Jack said to Kelly across the table. She continued to eat her breakfast and didn't look up from the paper.

"Kelly?" Jack asked, a laugh in his voice and a smile on his face. He reached across the table and covered her hand with his, rubbing her skin with his thumb.

"Hmm? Oh, me?" Kelly said looking up.

Jack laughed openly at that. Mabry listened to their exchange with a smug look on her face.

"Yes, you, my beautiful wife. I thought we might go to Le Petite Morceau for lunch today. They have a new chef who's supposed to be amazing. Unless you have plans?"

"Uh, no. I mean, no plans. I'd love to go to lunch," she said as she eyed Aunt Mabry nervously, knowing that Mabry was tracking every word, every interaction.

"Great," Jack smiled. "I have a conference call this morning, but I'll do that from home. We can go around one o'clock?"

"Perfect. I'll see you then," she said, but she felt like an idiot.

I'll see you then? Who the hell says that when their husband asks them to lunch? I sound like an idiot.

Mabry knew perfectly well as she watched Jack and Kelly that the two of them were no more married than she was, and she certainly wasn't married the last time she checked.

She didn't know what Kelly was getting out of this marriage—

she assumed it was money—but she could drive a wedge between them.

If she could put a big enough wedge there, maybe she could pay Kelly sufficient money to admit the marriage was fake. Once the marriage was exposed for what it was, Mabry would go to the board and show them their CEO was a fraud and a liar. And then, the company would be hers.

She went upstairs. It was time to split the happy couple up. It wouldn't be hard with all of Jack's exes out there. After all, the man was hardly the settling down type. Anyone who read the tabloids knew that he had a different woman on his arm every weekend.

Mabry picked up the phone and dialed Caroline Harridan. Caroline had dated Jack for a month the previous year, and Mabry knew she had done all she could to sink her claws into him. She wanted to marry Jack Sutton in the worst way, and Mabry had witnessed her throw herself at Jack repeatedly at public events since he broke up with her.

"Caroline? Hello, darling. It's Mabry Thompson," she said into the phone when Caroline answered.

"Mabry? How are you? I haven't heard from you in ages," she gushed on the other end of the phone.

Mabry rolled her eyes. Caroline fell all over herself whenever she talked to her, but Mabry knew it was an attempt to get information or back in Jack's good graces.

"Yes, dear. Well, you know. Been busy and all that," Mabry said dismissively. "I can't talk long because I have to meet Jack for lunch over at La Petite Morceau at one o'clock, and I have a million things to do before then. I thought I'd call and see how you are. It's been so long."

Mabry knew if she dropped the name of the restaurant and the time Jack would be there, she could count on Caroline to just 'happen' to be there as well. Mabry could sit back and let Caroline do the work for her.

"Oh!" Caroline practically squealed into her ear. "La Petite Morceau? I've been dying to try that place. I hear the new menu is to die for."

Mabry couldn't take Caroline's inane chattering or the sound of the woman's voice any longer. The seed was planted, and that was all that was needed.

"Caroline, I have to run. I've got to get to my hair appointment before lunch. It was lovely to talk with you again."

She couldn't get off the phone fast enough but if Caroline noticed, she didn't seem to mind. Mabry knew she was probably already in her closet picking out what to wear when she 'casually' ran into Jack at the restaurant.

CHAPTER 26

Kelly and Jack sat at a corner table at La Petite Morceau a few hours later. She looked around at the orchids on the tables and felt out of place in the upscale restaurant. She wasn't used to having lunch at a restaurant that had floor-length tablecloths and wait staff that wore ankle-long formal aprons.

Sure, she had been to that type of place for dinner on occasion, but not for lunch on a random Saturday when there was no special occasion to be celebrated.

She looked at Jack. He seemed totally at ease and comfortable... but then again, Jack always looked totally at ease and comfortable no matter where he was.

The only time she'd ever seen him looking the slightest bit uneasy was when she walked into his office and pretended to be his fiancée in front of his aunt and cousin—but even then, he covered his surprise easily and recovered quickly.

Kelly would love to be that confident and in control all of the time. With Jack around, she didn't feel confident or in control at all. She felt as if her body was constantly humming when she was around him.

One look from him, or a casual touch, and she was embarrassingly aroused. When he kissed her, she felt as if he could see into her and would know her secret—that she wanted him more than she had ever wanted any man.

Jack carried the conversation, chatting about the new menu and a fundraiser he attended at the restaurant when the old chef was there, and what they should do the rest of the weekend.

They ordered their meals, but just as they handed their menus over to the waiter, Kelly heard a sexy, sultry voice from across the room.

"My, my! Jack Sutton. Is that you, sweetheart?" said the voice at an embarrassingly loud volume. "I haven't seen you in ages, darling," Kelly heard as she watched a tall, blond goddess approach the table.

The woman was stunning, with exotic green eyes and her pale hair pulled in an elegant French twist. She wore a beautiful black pantsuit and looked as if she'd just stepped out of a fashion magazine.

She did a double take. The woman *had* stepped out of the pages of a fashion magazine. It was Caroline Harridan, the fashion model. The woman graced the pages of *Vogue* and *Elle* magazines on a regular basis.

Kelly looked at Jack as the stunning model approached their table and saw a pained look cross his face.

Caroline completely ignored Kelly as she swooped in on Jack and planted an extremely friendly kiss on his lips.

Kelly felt as though she were completely invisible and almost wished she was. They clearly had a relationship that was more than just friendly, and she knew she couldn't hold a candle to this woman as she sat there in her dowdy strappy sundress and sandals.

Kelly cleared her throat and peered around the woman to Jack.

He didn't miss a beat. "Caroline, you haven't met my wife, Kelly, yet have you? Kelly, this is Caroline Harridan. An old friend." He stood and came around to Kelly's seat as he made the introductions, so Kelly stood with him and took the other woman's hand in a brief handshake.

Jack looked as if the last thing he wanted to be doing was introducing Kelly as his wife, and once again she felt a pang of guilt at having put him in this position. Even though he said she was saving him from losing his company, she still felt as if she had weaseled her way into the marriage, and she knew she was nothing like the woman he would likely have married if he had been given a choice.

Nonetheless, Kelly drew up her pride and smiled her brightest smile. "It's a pleasure to meet you."

Caroline raised an eyebrow at Jack. God, Kelly had always wished she could master the one eyebrow look, but she couldn't quite get it. On Caroline, it looked confident, cocky, and oh so silky smooth.

"Married?" Caroline asked Jack as she drew her hand away from Kelly as if she were afraid she might be sullied by the contact.

Jack nodded and slipped his arm around Kelly. "Kelly and I were married a week ago. We haven't quite gotten around to sending an announcement out about the wedding. We eloped." He smiled down at Kelly as he said it in a very good impression of a man deeply in love with his wife.

Caroline pouted her best model pout. "Jack Sutton off the market? Whatever will all of us single gals do now?" She put on a show as if she were thinking and then shrugged her shoulders and continued in a flirty voice.

"Well, maybe it won't last." Caroline reached out and pretended to brush an imaginary piece of lint off of Jack's shirt in a blatant excuse to touch his chest. "You always know where to find me if things don't work out."

Kelly had now seen Jack uncomfortable twice since she'd

known him, but Caroline ignored his discomfort and Kelly's shocked look.

She couldn't believe what she was hearing. Hell, the marriage might be fake and she might not be able to compete with Jack's exes, including the blond goddess standing in front of her, but she'd be damned if she would sit by and let this woman hit on her fake husband right in front of her.

A woman has her pride, after all.

Kelly leaned in and possessively caressed Jack's chest in the very spot where Caroline's hand had just sat. "I'm sure Jack won't be needing your...." She paused and looked the other woman up and down as if she found her wanting in all manner before continuing, "Your...uh, company in the near future, Caroline. But it was a pleasure to meet you. Good-bye."

And with that, she dismissed Caroline Harridan, supermodel and cover girl.

Jack pulled Kelly tighter to him and Kelly could see him pressing his lips together.

In a huff, Caroline turned and stalked away from the table. As soon as they took their seats again, Kelly felt the heat climbing her cheeks.

"I'm so sorry," she whispered across the table to Jack.

"What for?" he whispered back, smiling.

"You probably wanted to see her again after this is over, and I think I must have ruined your chances for that. I just thought... Well, I couldn't. I mean, she was just so rude, I just...." She blew out a puff of air, blowing her bangs up in a small gust. "I'm sorry, I didn't think."

"Kelly, first of all, I'm married to you for the next year." Jack spoke quietly so no one would overhear their conversation. "I won't embarrass you or treat you with disrespect during that time. While we're together, we're together, and I won't be with another woman even if you and I aren't exactly together in the traditional sense."

He continued as she stared at him with wide eyes. "But second, that woman drives me up the wall. We went out a handful of times over the period of a month or so and she's stalked me ever since. Lord knows how she knew we were here today, but you can bet it wasn't a coincidence. She shows up at events and fundraisers and throws herself at me because she's determined to marry a wealthy man, and she couldn't care less that we had nothing in common and no spark whatsoever between us. You can chase her away any time you'd like," Jack finished with a smile and a wink at Kelly.

"Hmm," she said, frowning.

Jack laughed. "What now?"

"You didn't have a spark with *that*?" she asked, looking toward the door Caroline had walked out moments before. "How could you not sizzle with that?"

He looked at the door and back to Kelly and shrugged. "Just didn't. She's pretty vacant. A big old empty package with a huge bow, but not a damn thing inside the box."

CHAPTER 27

The following Monday, Kelly went shopping at the mall and then drove to New Haven to meet Jennie for lunch. Pulling her car into a space in the parking garage, she glanced in the rearview mirror before opening her car door to get out.

Kelly had a strange feeling that the car pulling past as she got out of her car was the same one behind her earlier that day at the mall. She watched as the car continued by and figured that she must be imagining things.

She walked through the parking garage and took the elevator down to the street level and went two doors along to the café where Jennie was waiting.

It had been a couple of weeks since she'd seen her friend, and they definitely needed to make up for lost time. She needed to fill in Jennie on her 'married' life with Jack, and she wanted to know how her friend's new job was going.

Kelly spotted Jennie at a table and pointed to the counter to signal that she'd grab a coffee and order lunch then join her. She ordered a turkey and avocado sandwich, picked up her iced coffee, and made her way over to the table.

Jennie's eyes immediately went to her left hand and the rather large diamond that sat alongside her wedding band. "He bought you an engagement ring?" she whispered in surprise as Kelly sat down.

"I know," she said and squirmed under Jennie's scrutiny. "I felt a little weird about it, but it was sweet, don't you think?"

"Very," said Jennie and she took Kelly's hand and examined the setting. "Tell me all about married life."

Kelly lowered her voice, not wanting anyone to hear the strange conversation they were about to have, given the state of her rather unconventional marriage. "He's actually really sweet. I mean, who would think that Jack Sutton would be sweet, right? We have dinner together almost every night. He asks about my day…. We watch movies or TV after dinner. It's nice, right?"

They paused while their sandwiches were delivered to the table.

Jennie watched Kelly for a minute as if reading the emotions on her friend's face. Her eyes were big and round, and she leaned in to whisper at Kelly. "Uh oh. You're falling for him a little, aren't you? You have a crush on your husband!"

"*Ugh*," Kelly said and rolled her eyes. "I am most definitely falling for him. His aunt moved into the house with us last Monday. She pretended it's because she's having work done on her townhouse, but we're pretty sure she's trying to prove the marriage is fake. That, of course, means we're sharing a room… and a bed."

"Oh boy, have you…?" asked Jennie as her eyes went even wider.

"No!" She shushed Jennie and looked around to be sure no one was listening. "No, I've been going to bed ridiculously early and pretending to be asleep when Jack comes in," she confessed with a grimace.

"Oh, God, you are not!" Jennie covered her mouth with her hand but couldn't cover the laughter. Kelly nodded and felt the now-familiar red heat creep into her cheeks.

When she recovered, Jennie pursed her lips and thought for a moment. "Well, you could go with it and have hot, wild monkey sex for a year with one of the hottest men on the continent."

Kelly laughed at her characterization of the situation but then dropped her smile. "No way. I couldn't do that. The guy dates supermodels and actresses with gorgeous, stick-thin bodies. I'd feel so stupid."

Jennie's normally fun demeanor was gone, and she put her coffee back down on the table and leaned toward Kelly. "Hey, you're gorgeous and you know it. He probably wants you already."

She gave a little shake of her head and smiled at her friend. "Uh uh. He just kisses me to keep up appearances. I'm no idiot, Jennie. I mean, don't get me wrong.... You know I've always liked the way I look. My body's not bad. But I'm no model. Let's face it —Jack Sutton is in a totally different universe in the looks department. He could easily be a model himself, and he dates models who wear a size two not ten."

"Don't knock the ten. Wasn't Marilyn Monroe a size ten or twelve? Something like that," Jennie grinned.

Kelly shook her head at her friend. She picked at her chips and then pushed her plate to the side and changed the subject. No matter how attractive he was, and how much they shared space, she was *not* going to throw herself at Jack; whether she was married to the man or not.

"Tell me about your new job. What do they have you doing now?" Kelly quickly changed the subject away from herself.

Jennie brightened and launched into the topic wholeheartedly. "It's great, actually. Whenever Sutton Capital is looking at investing in a company, they send someone from our office to do an audit. I go in with whoever we send and serve as their secretary for the time they're there. Then, I just work my magic.

"Sometimes it's a matter of people thinking I'm so innocent they forget not to talk in front of me. Or, I play up the ditz factor, and they just think nothing they tell me will matter. Other times, people end up opening up to me because they feel guilty about something they're not disclosing, so they want an outlet and they think it won't matter to tell me.

"So, even though they know I work for Sutton, they often seem to just open up and tell me stuff. Like, if there's any weakness in their company, or if they're hiding anything about their finances, or a problem with a patent, it has a way of coming out."

"Really?" Kelly asked. "They just tell you stuff even though they know it might hurt their chances of getting financing?"

"Yup. It's weird. Sometimes it's another secretary or support person and they want to gossip, but other times it's even the higher-ups that blurt stuff out. Chad says a lot of times, people are just looking to spill their guts, and they'll do it if you give them a chance. It's nice because I thought I'd have to lie to people and I was worried I would feel dishonest, but I don't even have to lie. I've only been on three assignments so far, but people just told me what we needed to know within days." Jennie seemed really happy with her new role.

Kelly grinned at her thinking back to Jennie's introduction of her and Jack. "It's not as if you're above a little spying now and again though, huh?"

Since Jennie couldn't deny it, all she could do was laugh and Kelly joined her, feeling better by the time they finished lunch.

Kelly walked out the front of the restaurant with Jennie after lunch.

"I never thought I'd say this, but good luck avoiding sex with your hot-as-hell husband," Jennie said with a smile.

Kelly laughed. "All right, I'll see you next week for lunch?"

As she dug in her purse for her car keys, she looked down the street past Jennie...and froze.

Kelly was absolutely sure that the car she had seen in the parking garage was now parked halfway down the block with a man sitting in it. He pulled out and turned at the corner, moving away from them, but she was positive this time it was the same car and the same man.

"Hey, Jennie," she said as she watched the car move away from them. "I think I'll walk up to Jack's office with you and stop in and say hi to him."

CHAPTER 28

Jack's new temp secretary had apparently been told who Kelly was because she sent her right into Jack's office. He smiled as she walked in, and she thought of the other time she'd been in his office and smiled back.

"Hi, sweetheart," he said as he wrapped his arms around her and kissed her, fusing his mouth to hers for more than just a little peck.

Kelly kicked herself for melting in his arms, and briefly noted he'd kissed her when there wasn't an audience that made it a necessity. She chalked it up to habit or as an unnecessary precaution on Jack's part and jumped into the reason for her visit.

"Um, Jack, I feel a little weird saying this, but I would swear someone was following me today," she said, biting her lip. Now that she was here, she felt a little silly telling him.

He apparently didn't think she was silly. He took Kelly by the shoulders and leaned down to look her directly in the eyes. "Tell me what you saw. Tell me everything you can remember," he said.

She was surprised at his response. She almost thought he'd tell her she was imagining things. Or at the very least that he'd try to reassure her and convince her it was nothing to worry about.

Kelly told him about the car and the man driving it. "It wasn't creepy like in a stalker, scary-guy kind of way. It was more like he was a private detective or professional kind of guy. "

She frowned. "Do you think your aunt is having me followed? Maybe she thinks she'll get proof that the marriage isn't real."

Jack considered this. "That's definitely a possibility. I wouldn't put it past her. I still don't like it, though. Do you have any ex-boyfriends or anyone who's ever bothered you in the past? Anything you can think of?"

She shook her head and shrugged. "No."

"I don't know," he said slowly. "I'm in the public eye a lot, but I've never had someone in my life that people know I care about. That might have made you a target for anyone who wanted to hurt me or wanted to get at my money. There might be more to this now that word about our marriage is getting around. I'll have security put on you."

Now that she had thought of the connection to Jack's aunt, Kelly felt a lot better about things and really thought they should turn this to their advantage. "No, no, no, Jack! I'm sure it's just your aunt. And, we can use this to our advantage. She isn't going to find anything. I mean, it's not as if I'm going to run out and sleep with some other guy or anything."

Kelly thought she saw Jack freeze for a split second when she said that, and wondered if he thought she was going to blow their cover by doing something that could prove their marriage wasn't real.

"Let her have me followed. The faster she sees that there isn't anything to dig up, the faster she'll back off and accept our marriage." Her enthusiasm for the idea increased the more she thought about turning the tables on Jack's Aunt Mabry.

As soon as Kelly said good-bye to Jack, promising to call him when she got back to the house, he got on the phone to Chad. He knew if he put a bodyguard with Kelly 24/7, it would scare her. He filled Chad in on the guy following Kelly without mentioning the possibility that it was Chad's mother who put the guy there. They talked about possible ways to protect Kelly, but Jack told Chad to keep her safe without scaring her too much.

Chad sent him a panic button with GPS that he'd have Kelly carry with her, and they settled on having one of Chad's people watch her from a block away at all times so they could get to her if she hit her panic button. With this in place they could watch her, but she wouldn't be frightened by the precautions. Chad also said he'd investigate the person tailing her and see what he could find out.

Jack felt better as he hung up the phone, but his response to the thought of someone threatening Kelly unnerved him. It was more than the ordinary level of protectiveness he expected to feel for her. It was a gut deep feeling of fear that something might happen to her.

Not something Jack was used to at all. And not something he liked.

CHAPTER 29

Andrew caught up to Kelly in the elevator. He'd seen her go into Jack's office and wanted a chance to talk to her.

She tucked her hair behind one ear nervously as he entered and pushed the button for the lobby.

He waited for the doors to slide shut before turning to her. "How's everything going? You settling in at Jack's"

"I am." The smile she gave him was tentative. "It's a beautiful house."

Andrew knew it was beautiful. He wondered if she would really be willing to give it up after a year. Prenuptial agreement or not, if she decided to fight Jack, she could easily threaten to go public with the agreement if Jack didn't let her stay. Or give her a big payoff. There were any number of ways this could go wrong.

"It is," he said as the elevator lowered. "Jack seems pretty happy with things. I take it everything is going well?"

As he said the words, he realized he'd really understated things. Jack had been more than happy lately. His friend seemed different. Relaxed. He was going home at a decent hour and more often than not, he had a smile on his face when he walked the halls of the company.

Hell, Andrew had walked into a negotiation the other day to

find Jack joking with the people across the table. That wasn't something that happened. Ever.

Kelly turned to Andrew, facing him fully and he saw the steel in her eyes this time. She might be nervous around him, but she apparently wasn't going to let that stop her speaking her mind.

"Mr. Weston, I appreciate that you're concerned about Jack and I'm glad he has a friend to watch his back like that, but I'm not going to talk to you about our marriage or his personal business."

Andrew's smile was slow but it was genuine. He wasn't willing to completely write off his concerns, but he liked that she would stand up for Jack that way and respect his privacy.

He nodded. "Good enough for me."

CHAPTER 30

Jack got home from work that night and slipped the panic button into Kelly's purse in the front hallway. She had started volunteering at the New Haven Legal Aid Clinic, and that wasn't located in the best part of town.

Between that and the guy following her, Jack felt better knowing she'd have some way of getting help if needed. He'd have to remember to tell her it was there and show her how to use it, but he didn't want to mention it in front of Aunt Mabry.

He walked into the kitchen and found Kelly and Mrs. Poole cooking dinner together. His wife looked up and smiled at him.

He thought she was gorgeous when she smiled at him like that, and he loved the sight of her in his kitchen. Hell, he loved coming home to find her anywhere in his house.

The irony of having the strongest feelings he'd ever had for a woman while in a fake marriage to her wasn't lost on Jack. He had spent years looking for the type of connection his mom and dad had shared, and now, when he finally gave up and entered into a fake marriage, he found himself looking smack at the woman he knew could have given him just what he had been looking for.

"Mrs. Poole is teaching me how to make her homemade

manicotti," Kelly said as she carefully placed a ricotta-filled noodle in a pan.

He inhaled a deep breath. The room smelled amazing and he knew the pot on the stove must contain Mrs. Poole's pasta sauce. It did something archaic to him to know Kelly was cooking for him. Neanderthal though that might be.

"I see," Jack said with a smile as he walked over and kissed her on the cheek, letting his mouth linger to take in her soft skin and the subtle scent of her.

She smiled at him before spooning the filling into the next noodle and rolling it up. He knew from experience they would fill the pan with the rows of noodles before layering sauce and cheese over it and baking it. The end result would be a gooey mess of cheese filled noodles drenched in mozzarella and sauce that he could never get enough of.

He could see Mrs. Poole's garlic bread already prepped on the counter, waiting to go into the oven. Perfect for sopping up the extra sauce and cheese.

"Maybe we can take a pan of it to your mom's house this weekend." He stayed close to her side, not wanting to put distance between them.

Kelly looked surprised that he was planning to go back to her parents' house with her this weekend, but before she could say anything his Aunt Mabry walked into the kitchen.

"I'm surprised to see you home so early in the evening, Jack," she said in her syrupy sweet voice that generally only came out when she was about to make a dig at someone. "I would've thought the CEO of a large company needs to work longer hours."

Biting back a sigh, Jack smiled at her. "Oh, I'll work a bit at home tonight, but I like to try to find a balance between work and home. That's how Dad always did it with Mom and me, and that's how I'll be now that I have my own family." He gave Kelly another squeeze around the waist as he said this, realizing he wished those words weren't based on a lie.

Kelly laughed and pushed him back spilling some of the ricotta filling over the edge of the noodle she was working on.

Jack saw a flicker of anger in Mabry's eyes, and he realized she probably hadn't seen much of his Uncle Dan in the evenings. Dan had worked a lot and was less of a family man than Jack's dad had been.

"Speaking of work, how long until dinner? I might as well go get some things done now," he said, turning to Kelly and Mrs. Poole. If he could finish up some of the things he need to take care of now, he would be able to spend more time with Kelly that evening.

It was Mrs. Poole who answered. "About an hour, dear," she said in her mothering tone.

The endearment earned a hard look from Aunt Mabry.

"Call me when it's ready?" Jack grabbed an apple from the fruit basket on the counter and tossed it in the air as he walked out of the kitchen toward his home office.

Even with Mabry doing all she could to make their lives miserable, he was happier than he could remember being in a long time.

After dinner, Jack suggested they sit on the patio to watch the stars. Mrs. Poole went into the kitchen to clean up while Mabry, Jack, and Kelly went outside with a bottle of wine and three glasses.

Aunt Mabry and Jack sat in Adirondack chairs on the patio while Kelly poured the wine and lit the three squat candles sitting on a low glass table between the chairs. Jack took his glass from Kelly, looped an arm around her waist and pulled her down onto his lap.

She squawked at the move and he felt her tense briefly, but then she relaxed into him and he grinned.

He knew he was getting to her as much as she was getting to him. Jack worried for a minute that it might be cruel to tease her as much as he did, but he quickly dismissed the thought. It was fun and he loved making her blush and squirm. Reluctance from a woman wasn't something he was used to, but damn, it was like an aphrodisiac.

Jack kept his arms around Kelly's waist and his hands rested on her tummy, but as they drank their wine and made idle conversation with his aunt, he found one hand moving just high enough on her stomach to let him brush his thumb back and forth on the lower curve of her incredible, full breast.

He meant to do it to torment Kelly, but it backfired on him as he found himself burning with heat for her.

Fuck.

He wasn't focusing on a word Mabry was saying and judging by the way Kelly's breath caught, he didn't think she was either. If Mabry noticed neither of them was talking to her, she didn't show it.

Why the hell was his aunt out here with them anyway? He willed her to go back inside the house.

Or maybe he could convince Kelly to go inside with him? They could say they were tired and go up to their room. To their bed.

Damn the thought had him hard as a rock.

Jack took his other hand and brushed the hair back from her neck, pushing it to one side as he leaned over her shoulder to speak so that his words caused his breath to brush against her soft skin.

He didn't get a word out before Kelly sprang from his lap.

"I, uh, I'm going to go for a run. Forgot to do my workout today," she said, pulling the excuse out of thin air.

Jack was fairly sure she hadn't gone for a run the whole time she'd lived there.

"I'll, um, I'll see you guys later," she said as he grinned at her and stifled a laugh.

Mabry shook her head as she watched Kelly walk away.

"She's an odd one, Jack," Mabry said.

Jack grinned. "One of a kind Aunt Mabry. One of a kind."

CHAPTER 31

Jack waited in his home office, keeping busy as he looked at projections and company profiles until he heard Kelly come in from her run and start the shower. He'd sent Mrs. Poole off to her apartment early and his aunt was out for the evening.

He climbed the stairs and headed for their bedroom, opening the French doors that led to the balcony and leaning on the railing while he waited for her to finish.

This was going to be fun, he thought. A lot of fun.

He heard the shower turn off and turned to wait for her to open the door.

If he thought he was prepared for what he saw, he was dead wrong.

Kelly stepped out moments later with her hair hanging wet over her shoulders, wearing nothing more than a towel wrapped around her. She'd tucked an end into the dip between her breasts to hold it up and the alluring picture that presented, as though she was there for him to unwrap, hit him hard.

He was actually stunned silent for a minute and stared as she crossed the room to the walk-in closet without realizing he was in the room watching her.

He had known Kelly was gorgeous and the slight touches they'd shared over the past weeks had teased him, but seeing her like this was so much more than he imagined. He felt a jolt straight down to his groin and swallowed as he watched her.

Creamy skin that looked so soft he was dying to nibble every inch of it taunted him. Her breasts were full and begged for his hands to hold them, his tongue to explore them. The towel fell just past luscious hips that curved and cried out to be held, explored, entered.

He damned near groaned out loud at the thought.

Her legs were smooth and bare and still had small droplets of water on them that shimmered against her skin. Jack could picture himself covering those legs from her ankles to thigh with slow, lazy kisses.

Kelly turned and saw Jack watching her from the balcony, and her small scream jolted him back to his senses. A slow smile spread across his face, but his eyes burned hot and intense as he watched her.

Kelly pulled the towel tighter around her curves as he walked slowly over to join her.

"Why are you avoiding me in the evenings, Kelly?" he asked her softly wanting an answer to his question now more than ever.

Kelly felt as if Jack's low, gravelly voice were washing over her, caressing her. Her body tingled in anticipation.

"I-I...." She stumbled over her words and couldn't come up with more to say as he slowly stalked toward her.

He moved in on her, and she had to back up against the wall to keep some distance between them. When she couldn't go any further, Jack leaned down and kissed the curve between her neck and her shoulder, lingering as his breath tickled and teased her.

She felt her body go soft and warm for him, the apex of her

legs seeming to heat in anticipation of his touch. Her breath caught in her chest and her heart fluttered wildly.

"You're avoiding me, Kelly." Jack pressed hot kisses down her shoulder. "What I can't figure out is why you would do that because I know you're as attracted to me as I am to you."

Now he looked at her as she shook her head, causing him to grin in response. It was a feral grin. One that promised retribution for the lie.

"Kelly, it's my job to know when people are bluffing," he said as he ran the tips of his fingers lightly over her arms, down to her wrists and back up again.

The touch set her on fire.

"You're bluffing, Kel. You're attracted to me. I feel it when I kiss you, when you press your body against mine, when your breath hitches as I whisper in your ear."

Kelly's head swam, and she could barely think straight as Jack attacked all of her senses. "No, I'm not. I mean, I'm...."

Frustrated, she felt the heat creep up her cheeks as she tried to explain why she had avoided this very scene. She needed to make him understand without humiliating herself.

"Jack, I'm not like the women you've been with. I'm not a supermodel. I'm just normal. Completely normal with a normal body and normal breasts, and I wear normal size clothes not Barbie Doll sizes like you're used to."

Once Kelly got started, she blurted it all out.

"I can't compete with what you're used to. I don't want to compete with them."

Jack stopped his seductive teasing and stood up and she would swear he was stunned. Now he leveled a look at her.

"You're completely serious, aren't you? You don't think I'm attracted to you." He didn't back off an inch. He kept her pressed against the wall.

"It's okay, Jack. I mean, I didn't expect you to be when we

started this, and I'm okay with that." Kelly continued to babble on as he watched her in disbelief.

"Then, I'll have to convince you." He dipped a finger into the vee of Kelly's towel at her breasts and tugged her gently toward him as he captured her mouth with his once again. When he broke from her lips, leaving her breathless, he looked her in the eyes again.

"I'm extremely attracted to you, Kelly. I love your body. I love your curves, the size of you, your softness, your full breasts—everything about you. All you have to do is enter the room and I'm ready for you. And soon, I'm going to convince you of that and get you into bed in the true sense instead of just sleeping next to me."

As Jack spoke, he peppered her neck, shoulders, mouth, and jawline with searing kisses that had Kelly's legs shaking and her body melting for him.

"And when I take you to bed, Kelly, you'll be confident that I'm truly interested in being there with you—and nobody else. That I want to be there with *you*."

He ravaged her mouth with one last deep kiss, drawing it out before he released her.

"Good night, sweetheart," he said, and he smiled at her dazed expression as he slipped from the room.

CHAPTER 32

The following afternoon, Kelly received two dozen deep-red roses that were so incredibly beautiful they took her breath away. The card read: *Like your lips—lush and full and sensual. Have a wonderful day, beautiful.*

Mrs. Poole and Mabry read the card over her shoulder. Mrs. Poole sighed at the romance of the gesture; Mabry huffed and walked away.

The following day, Kelly came home to find a large bouquet of blush roses laced with baby's breath. Mrs. Poole and Mabry waited for her in the front hall to read the card. *The color of your cheeks when I make you blush only makes me want to do it more.*

Mrs. Poole sighed and Mabry harrumphed and walked away again. Kelly blushed.

The next day, she couldn't help but hurry home from the clinic to see if more flowers had arrived. She wasn't disappointed. A dozen bright orange gerbera daisies sat in the front hall.

"Oh! I love gerbera daisies," she exclaimed. "They always make me smile."

"What did he do wrong?" Mabry asked.

Kelly ignored her as she opened the card and laughed at the

message: *This is what your smile does for me. It feels like sunshine and happiness and having a home after a long time without one.*

The next day she came home to a stunning orchid with the most unique white and purple blooms on a tall stem. It wasn't like any orchid she had seen before and the card read: *A bloom that is rare and stunning with taunting curves that demand to be explored, just like you.*

Kelly was sure she might have heard Mabry sigh. She definitely heard one from Mrs. Poole.

Friday was a vase of blue and yellow irises with a card that read: *I tried to find a flower that was as beautiful as the stunning blue of your eyes, but there wasn't anything that came close. You're one of a kind.*

Mrs. Poole had to dry a tear, and Kelly was sure this time she heard a small sigh escape from Aunt Mabry's lips before she pressed them tightly closed and walked away.

Later that day, cream-colored roses arrived with a note that read: *Dinner tonight? I'll pick you up at six o'clock.*

Jack knew the sentiments and notes were cheesy, each and every one of them, but he also knew Kelly would eat it up, and he smiled when he imagined her reaction to them.

And every night when he came home, she blushed and thanked him before he pulled her to him for a kiss.

Making Kelly blush was one of his favorite things, and he fully planned to make her blush in their bed soon, too.

CHAPTER 33

Jack and Kelly pulled up to the valet at a wine bar in downtown New Haven. Phase two of what Jack had dubbed Project Kelly was a night out with an intimate dinner followed by a show at the Yale Repertory Theater.

Jack thought she would like the cozy restaurant and the unassuming theater instead of the big flashy events they sometimes had to attend for his business. He wanted her to relax with him and feel comfortable so he could spend the night showing her how much he wanted her, how much she did for him by being there when he came home each night.

Jack watched as Kelly walked into the restaurant. There was nothing assuming or arrogant about her. Everywhere she went, eyes were on her, yet she seemed totally oblivious. She didn't preen or even try to draw more attention to herself. There wasn't anything conceited about her and that made her all the more appealing.

She wore a deep blue dress with thin straps that showed off her creamy soft shoulders. She'd pulled her hair up which he quickly discovered he loved because it let him see the delicate curve of her neck. He couldn't help but fantasize about nibbling the smooth skin or trailing his lips over it and making her moan.

Jack was far from oblivious to the attention being paid to Kelly as she walked past other patrons. He wanted to rip the eyes out of every man there and save her all for himself. He pushed down that urge and satisfied himself with a few warning looks at the worst of the oglers, and placed a possessive hand at the small of her back as they followed the maitre d' to their table.

The light contact of Jack's hand on her back sent tingles down her spine all the way to her toes. After his announcement that he planned to prove how attracted he was to her, Kelly had been unable to stop thinking about the hungry way he had looked at her, the way he looked at her as if he were stalking his next meal.

Maybe it should have made her feel like a piece of meat, but it didn't. It made her feel desirable, wanted in a way no other man had made her feel. She began to believe Jack when he said he wanted her.

As they sat down at the table, Kelly felt Jack's eyes on her and realized he hadn't picked up his menu. He just stared at her.

"You look amazing tonight," he said, and she was glad she had swept up her hair and worn a spaghetti strap dress that showed off her shoulders.

She imagined what it would feel like to have Jack kiss her neck, her shoulders, even outline the thin straps of her dress with his tongue as he worked his way down to her breasts, searing her skin with each hot touch.

She blushed as her thoughts sent heat coursing through her body. "Thank you," she said quietly.

Jack gave her a puzzled look. "You know something I like about you, Kelly?" he asked her quietly, but didn't wait for an answer. "You honestly don't seem to know how stunning you are or how much you affect me. It's really not an act with you." Jack shook his head.

Before she could get her voice back, the waiter was at the table and Jack turned to listen politely to the specials. Kelly tried to listen to the waiter, but all she could do was think about Jack and the effect his words had on her.

Kelly realized the waiter was asking her if she'd like a drink. Pulling herself out of her thoughts, she ordered a glass of Pinot Noir and opened her menu. When the waiter came back with their drinks a few minutes later, they each ordered the beef tenderloin—and crab cakes to split as an appetizer.

"So, why law school?" Jack asked Kelly while they waited for their food.

"When I was in high school, my best friend's dad was indicted on money-laundering charges. He decided to take a plea deal because the prosecution said they had some other charges they could bring if he didn't agree to a deal, and he knew a trial would have been long and brutal on his family. He was innocent of the charges; we all knew it and believed in him, but he said he couldn't risk going to jail longer than he would if he agreed with the plea bargain. He wouldn't put his family through the ordeal of a trial or a longer sentence," she explained and sipped her wine.

They both paused as the waiter put their appetizer down.

"What happened to him?" Jack asked, offering Kelly a crab cake.

"Well, when it came time to enter the plea bargain, Judge Thomas, the judge presiding over the case, said that he thought something wasn't right with the case. He spent the whole week listening to the taped evidence the prosecution had based their case on. He scoured the tapes and poured through eyewitness reports and evidence that supposedly showed our friend's guilt. He didn't need to be that thorough, but he was.

"Based on what he discovered, he set aside all of the charges at the last minute instead of sentencing him to prison as the plea would have required. The judge said that there was no evidence to show any wrongdoing, and the evidence showed that the eyewitnesses were conspiring to frame him for the crimes because they had a personal vendetta against him and his family. It was this huge drama, and everyone was stunned when the judge announced it, but I remember sitting there and feeling in awe of this judge and the system and the way he stood up for this guy and made sure that the right thing happened."

"I think I remember that from the papers," Jack said. "I met Judge Thomas once at a fundraiser for a charity I'm involved with. He was the keynote speaker. I remember every person I spoke with about him or saw him interact with had a lot of respect for him."

"What charities do you work with?" Kelly seized on his charity work, happy to find out more about Jack.

"Well, right now, I'm on the boards of two. One that provides funding for children who need major surgery and don't have the insurance or means to pay for it. That's the one I do the most work for because it's still growing. We're trying to expand to offer assistance to more children, and to be able to offer assistance for cosmetic surgeries as well as medical surgeries so that we can help children with deformities or with scarring, that type of thing. I've been working to drum up funds from my investors."

"Wow," said Kelly. "That sounds like a great charity. What's the other one?"

She was surprised to see Jack look a little hesitant, as if he didn't want to admit what the other charity was. She seemed to be surprised more and more by him lately.

"It's a rescue organization for dogs. It focuses on rescuing mixed-breed dogs and re-homing them. I'm not as involved in that one though. I've never really had time for a dog of my own, so I wanted to do something for dogs. I guess I keep thinking things will slow down and I'll adopt a dog, but they never seem to. Slow down, I mean. Probably my fault," he said grinning. "I tend to be a workaholic."

"You aren't too bad about work," Kelly said, looking at him across the now empty appetizer plate. "I mean, sure, you go in early, but you're home every evening by a decent hour."

"Oh, that's new. I've only started doing that since you moved in," Jack said.

Kelly frowned. "You don't need to change things for me, Jack. I never meant to keep you from your work."

He grinned at her over the table. "I like it, Kelly. I like coming home at a normal hour and having time for dinner with you. I think it's a good change."

"Oh," she said, the surprise on her face likely clear to him. "Oh," she said more quietly to herself, and Jack laughed as she processed his confession. She didn't really know how to feel about it.

After they enjoyed their meal and several glasses of wine, and split a dish of chocolate mousse, they decided to walk around the green before going over to the theater. Jack took Kelly's hand in his, causing a flood of warmth through her body.

She liked that he didn't seem to need to fill the silence as they walked. If they ran into a lull in the conversation, they could just leave it there, comfortable not to fill all the gaps with nonsense or babbling.

They talked more about Kelly's plans for law school and her hope to work in appellate law after she graduated. Jack also updated her on some of the more interesting projects at work.

They laughed at Aunt Mabry's blatant efforts to investigate their marriage, and Jack told her how Andrew nearly choked when Jack told him about Kelly's big entrance the day they got engaged at his office.

CHAPTER 34

Jack and Kelly stopped to look at a church that sat along the edge of the green. It was an old stone church with one whole wall filled with stained glass windows. There were five tall panels in striking blue and teal, with reds mixed throughout and a circle above the panels in matching colors.

Even from the outside of the building it was breathtaking, and Jack wondered what it would look like from the inside with the sun streaming into the building. A small marker told them that the shape of the window was known as a chrysanthemum window.

As they stood looking up at the church windows, Jack wrapped his arms around Kelly from behind and pulled her close to him, resting his chin on the top of her head. He dipped his head to her neck and nuzzled her soft skin, enjoying the feel of her softness against him and the sweet smell of her.

She always smelled so good, and he wondered if it was a perfume or just an exceptional combination of her shampoo and innate sweetness.

Kelly tilted her head and opened her neck to him, and he kissed a trail across the back of her neck as he slowly enjoyed the feel of her skin on his lips. Her skin was soft and warm and it made him linger to feel her more.

He leisurely worked his way up to one ear, where he tugged her earlobe with his teeth before he caressed the same lobe with his lips to soften the bite. Kelly moaned and dipped her head.

He turned her in his arms and kissed along the soft line of her jaw, then slowly worked his way to her mouth, with sweet, soft kisses. When he got to her mouth, he abandoned the gentleness and covered her supple mouth with his.

Kelly responded to him, rising up on her toes to get closer to him. Her small fists closed in on his shirt, and she gripped the fabric over his hard chest the way they had when he kissed her under the tree in her parents' yard, but this time she didn't stop, but kept pulling him closer, sending Jack's body into overdrive.

His tongue swept into her mouth, first entering to play with the tip of her tongue, then plunging deeper. Kelly pressed her body against the hardness of Jack's chest and torso, and he felt her nipples brush against him sending a rush to his groin. He wanted to lay her down in the grass and feel every inch of her heated skin on his, to bury himself in her curves.

Jack ended the kiss, but held his forehead to hers as he caught his breath for a minute. "Sorry," he said, his voice raw. "I forgot for a minute that we were in a public park."

"Mm hmm," said Kelly as if she didn't trust herself with words.

He chuckled. "Maybe we should skip the show? I can always get us tickets for another time."

Kelly nodded, and they turned to walk back to the car.

Neither of them noticed the dark sedan pull out from the curb as they walked away.

CHAPTER 35

The thirty-minute car ride seemed to Kelly like it took forever. They rode in silence but it was a comfortable silence, and she laughed as he pushed the speed limit, trying to shave off the minutes to get them home and up to their room.

His hand lingered on her thigh and his thumb brushed back and forth sending small shivers through her body with each teasing movement.

Kelly couldn't believe that Jack had been telling the truth. She could feel his attraction for her as much as she could feel the pull of temptation to him. When he had her in his arms, she felt beautiful, desirable and wanted—beyond words.

Jack pulled his car into the driveway and came around to open her door. He offered her his hand and pulled her into his arms for a kiss before he turned toward the house without releasing her hand.

Minutes later, they walked into their bedroom and Jack pulled her into his arms.

"Have I told you how incredible you look tonight?" he asked.

Kelly laughed. "You mentioned it once or twice, but I don't think you can overdo that. Have I told you how handsome you are tonight?" she asked as she ran her hands up the hard muscles of his biceps and onto his strong, broad shoulders. She could feel the power of his body beneath the soft, textured fabric of his shirt and she felt fragile in his arms.

Kelly pressed her palms flat against Jack's shoulders and ran her fingers down his chest. She luxuriated in the feel of him and spread her fingers to try to feel more, to feel it all. Touching Jack made her hands tingle, sent a rush of heat through her body, sent a tightening ache down her belly and through her thighs in anticipation of what would come.

∼

Jack looked into her eyes until he didn't think he could stand it anymore, then dipped his head to capture her lips. Kelly gasped and sank further into him, pressing her body to his.

He reached behind her, unzipped her dress and it fell in a puddle at her feet. He let out a long, low groan at the sight of her, as his eyes traveled from her breasts down the smooth skin of her belly to her thighs, and all the way down her sexy legs, marveling at the creamy texture of her skin.

Jack dropped to his knees, his hands on her hips, mouth brushing softly on her belly, worshiping her as she let out a soft moan. He looked up to find her watching him, and the image of her eyes on him as he kissed her sent new waves of arousal through him as more blood rushed to his insistent erection.

Kelly was sexy and alluring and powerful standing above him as if all doubts about her beauty had been washed away. She reached down and pulled him up to stand before her and began to unbutton his shirt. She moved slowly.

Jack watched her small hands work the buttons of his shirt. But when she finished and reached in to touch his chest, it felt as if her fingers would burn him. He scooped her up and brought her to the bed, then stood watching her as he removed the rest of his clothing.

"I've never seen anyone as gorgeous as you look lying in my bed, Kelly," he said. He brought his body down on top of hers and pressed lightly down on her as he kissed her lips once more before moving to the bottom of the bed.

"So beautiful." Jack kissed her ankles.

"So sexy." He traced kisses up her calves, along her thighs, all the while running one hand up her hips and into the curve of her waist and back down the full length of her legs.

"So soft."

CHAPTER 36

Jack made Kelly feel cherished and treasured. Her body tingled as he touched her and she wanted so much more.

He left her legs and moved to her breasts. She sighed as he undid the small clasp in the front of her bra to cup her breasts in his hands. He let the skin on his palms play across her nipples, teasing them and bringing them to life for him.

He pulled her right nipple into his mouth, circled it gently with his tongue, and then sucked and nipped at it with his teeth before moving to the left breast, causing heat to pool in between Kelly's legs.

Kelly pulled Jack up and kissed him. She wrapped her arms and legs around him, pulling him closer, needing to feel him pressed against her. She needed him closer still. She pressed her body into his and arched her back, desperate to feel all of him.

"Please, Jack," she begged softly, and she felt his smile against her lips in answer.

"Not yet, Kelly." His voice was low and raw, and his words sent shivers of anticipation up and down her spine as she writhed and moaned beneath him. Her body felt like an instrument that no one had known how to play before Jack. As his hands played over her body, she came alive.

Jack slid his hand between her legs to slip his hand under the silk and lace of her panties. She was wet and ready for him, swollen and hot.

"Jack." His name slipped from her lips as if on a prayer.

He peeled Kelly's panties down her hips and off her legs then returned to the head of the bed once again. He pinned her wrists above her head with one hand and continued his torturous, slow exploration, this time between her legs.

Kelly writhed beneath his hand and pressed herself into him, whimpering with desperate need. He teased her until she bucked under his hand and begged him to relieve her aching need.

He moved his fingers over her faster, giving her the speed and pressure she needed to reach her orgasm, and didn't let up until he felt her break into pieces in his arms.

Jack held her while she caught her breath, then reached into the bedside drawer for a condom and quickly put it on. He lay on top of her and pressed himself against her, not entering her yet, but teasing, taunting, building her up again.

Kelly was wide-eyed with surprise as she arched against him and strained to get him to enter her, to end the torture.

With one swift stroke, Jack slid inside and they both cried out at the sensation of her wrapping around him, gripping him. He held still inside her for a moment, but she could only stay still for so long. She started to move her hips in tiny circles, pulling forth another groan from Jack as he began to slide in and out of her, slowly burying himself deeper within her.

Kelly tightened her legs around him and moved as he did. She pushed toward him and brought him deeper still. Jack wrapped one arm around her waist as he felt her body tense—coiling as if ready for release.

He leaned in to kiss her neck, and drove into her again and again as she began to shatter and pulse around him. Kelly fisted her hands into Jack's hair and cried out his name as wave upon wave of sweet release rolled over her.

He continued to move slowly inside her, and she could feel the sweet, aching pleasure as it built in her again. She ran her hands up and down Jack's chest.

She wanted to feel every ounce of him as she tightened her muscles around him and marveled at the feel of him tight inside her, hard and smooth and filling her. She brought her mouth to his and kissed him, then bit his lower lip before she gently soothed the hurt with her tongue.

Jack moved inside Kelly, marveling at the feel of her muscles wrapped tightly around him sharing her every response with him, her arms grasping him for more.

He tried not to think about the fact that every moment with her was better than the last, that everything about making love with Kelly was so much different, so much better than it was with any of the women he had taken to bed in the past.

She whispered, "Deeper, Jack," into his ear and the sound of the whispered demand in her soft, sweet voice pushed him right over the edge. She fell along with him and rode the waves of her orgasm until he collapsed on top of her, both of them completely sated.

CHAPTER 37

Kelly smiled to herself as she realized where she was and whose arms were holding her. She could feel Jack stirring, and his hands began to slide over her body as she pressed greedily up against him. She stretched the length of her body against Jack, trying to feel more of him, all of him.

"Good morning, beautiful," he whispered as he trailed kisses along her shoulder. She had no idea that sensations on her shoulders could be so erotic, so sensitive, and if she were forced to pick a favorite spot at the moment, her shoulders might just be it.

Jack rolled her to face him and moved down her neck to the hollow between her breasts, and she thought briefly that she might need to change that assessment. When he took one nipple into his mouth and swirled his tongue over its peak, she knew she would never be able to choose a favorite. Everywhere Jack touched her, she felt on fire.

Kelly pressed against him, wanting to feel him inside her again. She ran her hands down his chest and around to his back and marveled at the feel of his muscles, the smooth coolness of his skin under her hands, the hard tautness of his muscles rippling under the surface. It only took a small touch of his body to have her not only ready for him, but willing to plead with him to take her.

With one swift move, Jack flipped them over so that he was lying on his back and Kelly straddled him. She laughed and smiled down at him.

"Good morning, Jack." She began to rub herself along his hard length, but she didn't take him into her yet.

Jack groaned and tried to pull her down onto him, but she laughed and pulled back.

Kelly thrilled to the feeling of power, her ability to bring this incredible man to his knees. She rocked her hips back and forth and enjoyed the slick, wet, hard feel of him between her legs slipping back and forth in her folds.

Jack watched Kelly's face as she writhed above him. It was sheer torment not to slide inside her, but he could see now that she was close to the brink and he watched her face, in awe of her beauty as she brought herself closer and closer to climax on him.

It was incredible to see her so powerful, taking what she wanted from him, and he gritted his teeth to hold out long enough for her as she suddenly cried out and came crashing down.

She pulsed with pleasure, and Jack held her as the waves rode through her. When her body finally relaxed, he put one arm around her waist and flipped her underneath him in one quick motion.

She let out a giggle, but that quickly turned to a moan as he slipped on a condom and entered her in a swift thrust, and plunged into her depths, again and again until he found his own release with Kelly wrapped around him, holding him as he buried himself deeper inside her than she'd thought possible.

Collapsing in a heap, he pulled her tight into his arms, and they fell asleep once again.

CHAPTER 38

Jack cradled Kelly as they lay lazily in bed, her head on his chest, while one of his hands drew languid circles on her shoulders and neck. He had never much cared to snuggle with women in the past, but he couldn't seem to get enough of Kelly. He was compelled to hold her and touch her in whatever way he could until his body had recharged enough to take her again.

He loved the feel of her skin on his hands, the brush of her breath on his chest, the way their legs tangled together or her hair tickled his skin and teased him to life again.

He closed his eyes, content to hold her in his arms as long as she would let him.

"Jack?"

"Hmm?" Jack's hand didn't stop its exploration of Kelly's soft skin as he answered her.

"Why is your aunt so dead set on having Chad in charge?" she asked, not lifting her head from where she was snuggled into Jack's side.

"To hurt me." He paused before adding, "There was a time when she was the happiest woman you've ever seen. Hell," Jack said on a laugh, "she used to be as happy as Mrs. Poole."

Kelly raised her eyebrows at that but waited for Jack to continue.

"Our families used to be so close. Chad and I were both only children, so he and I grew up more as brothers than cousins. We went on family vacations together, saw each other all the time. In those days, Aunt Mabry was so much fun. She was like a second mom to me. Then, one day, my uncle left her. He left, and we hardly see him. Even Chad hardly hears from him. He didn't leave for another woman or anything like that. Chad said she felt like she wasn't good enough, that he thought being alone was better than being with her. I thought he was a selfish prick, but what do I know?"

Jack shrugged. "First she was sad all the time, but over time she seemed to be angry with everyone around her. A lot of it was focused on my mom and dad. I think she couldn't stand to be around them.

"Luckily, by the time she focused on me, Chad and I were adults so it didn't affect our friendship or working relationship. She comes off as this obnoxious, mean person now, but she really isn't. She's just hurting."

"I like that family is more important to you than anything else," Kelly said. "Besides, your Aunt Mabry is the reason you're putting me through law school if you think about it, so I'm okay with her craziness." She grinned, and Jack let out a laugh and held her closer.

He could get used to this. Hell, forget getting used to it. He could come to crave it. Need it.

He closed his eyes and focused on what they had together. The here and now.

CHAPTER 39

The man in the black sedan watched Kelly as she parked her car and entered the legal aid clinic. So far, she hadn't spotted him. Just like all the other women he'd been sent to sit on, she seemed oblivious to everything around her. Fucking clueless.

As the door closed behind her, he hit the speed dial on his phone and waited, listening to the ringing sound in the earpiece. He knew they'd pick up quickly. They were eager to get this one done.

"It's me," he said when the call connected.

"Have you found a pattern yet?" asked the voice on the other end of the phone.

He spoke again. "She doesn't seem to have many regular routines other than coming to the clinic on East Street. No regular job, no schedule for shopping or working out that I can see. She's often with her husband or one of her friends, but she comes to the clinic every morning, and she's alone then. That's her only steady commitment."

"We'll grab her there, then," the voice said, cold, calculated, without feeling. There was a reason this asshole was in charge. He didn't give a fuck. Not a scrap of remorse in him.

"There's another problem. They've put security on her. They don't stay right on her, but they're nearby at all times." The man hesitated watching the tail the woman had on her a block up the way. He didn't have a good feeling about this. "I think we should ditch her. Find a replacement."

There was silence on the line and he knew he'd stepped in it, but fuck, it was gonna be his ass on the line if this shit went sideways. No one else would get hauled in with him. And he wouldn't talk. He wasn't a fucking rat.

"I just mean, uh," he said, trying to back himself out of it. "I just thought we should be sure. There are other brunettes who fit the look."

"No," came the response from the other end, an edge to it that made him shift in his seat. "She's the one. I've already sent a preview to our buyers. Send someone into the clinic so we have a friendly face close to her. We'll get her away from her security and lure her out."

Kelly's days were starting to fill up. She went to the legal aid clinic routinely every morning and stayed until noon. She helped people fill out the necessary paperwork and matched them with the right attorney for their problem. The process gave her a chance to see a pretty wide range of legal issues and get an idea of what types of problems people faced.

She was also getting to meet a lot of the attorneys around New Haven because the clinic pulled volunteers from the major firms around town who were looking for a way to fulfill their law firms' pro bono requirements.

Once or twice when she left the clinic, Kelly was fairly sure she saw the all-too-familiar dark sedan turn a corner or sit idling a block away. She knew Mabry's investigator wasn't going to find any dirt on her, though, so she ignored the car and its driver pretending she hadn't seen them.

Now that she was spending time in New Haven at the clinic, she met Jack for lunch whenever he could get away from work. They decided to try to work their way through every New Haven restaurant they could, and one day Jack even surprised her by having Mrs. Poole pack a picnic lunch to eat out on the green. She laughed when he tried to take credit for preparing the meal himself, knowing full well that he had never lifted a cooking utensil in his life.

On Friday, she and Mabry took the train into the city and found a cocktail dress for the party Jack and Kelly were hosting. The designer's name meant nothing to her, but Mabry was impressed by it. More importantly, Kelly liked the dress. It was silky midnight black with an A-line skirt that flared around her thighs. Swarovski crystals sprinkled like raindrops from waist to hem, and the spaghetti straps were also dotted with tiny, sparkling crystals.

The saleswoman was right; it did show off Kelly's hourglass figure and generous curves, and she ended up feeling very sexy when they paired it with silver strappy heels and smoky charcoal-gray undergarments edged with raspberry red lace.

Kelly tried to see signs of the Aunt Mabry that Jack had told her about, but all she could see was her pinched face and scheming mind. She felt sad for Mabry, really.

Not sad because her husband had left her, but sad that she couldn't let it go—that it still affected her so badly. She didn't get the sense it was because Mabry had loved her husband.

It seemed as though the woman's pride was hurt, and she couldn't get past the anger of that. Kelly wondered what it would be like to hold on to anger for that long.

Still, as much as she felt for the woman, she couldn't say she enjoyed the end-of-week shopping trip at all.

On Saturday evening, Jack said he had a surprise for her. He told her he was sure she was going to love it and he was right. They enjoyed a five-star dinner served on a private boat out on the sound prepared by a five-star chef.

As the water rocked them and they looked up at the stars, Kelly couldn't imagine anything more romantic. She was once again hit with a sharp pain when she remembered that their life together was based on a contract and nothing more. That this was a temporary deal. A temporary deal with a very definite and looming expiration.

CHAPTER 40

On Sunday morning, Jack walked into the kitchen to find Kelly cooking breakfast. It was Mrs. Poole's day off, and Aunt Mabry was still in bed. He stifled a groan as he watched Kelly bend over to dig for a pan in the cabinet under the stove.

She was wearing an old pair of boxers and a T-shirt, but she couldn't be sexier...and the way the boxers stretched tight over her bottom when she bent over made him want to skip breakfast and find out how sturdy his kitchen table was.

He stood enjoying the curve of her calves; imagining his hands on her thighs, pressing his fingers into her hips as he pulled her tight to him. Within seconds, his own pants were tight, and he was very happy that Mrs. Poole took Sundays off.

The longer he stood there, the more he realized he didn't want this to end any time soon. He liked having Kelly around the house. He liked spending time with her and making her smile and laugh. He liked spoiling her with presents, and he liked finding new ways to make her scream out his name in bed.

Maybe he could ask her to stay through law school. It wouldn't hurt her to have a home to live in and Mrs. Poole to take care of her while she got her degree. And then there was the bar exam to study for and maybe a clerkship to get through....

Before he knew it, Jack was wondering if he could convince Kelly to continue their arrangement for another five years or so. What could he offer her to convince her to stay?

He'd have to make it worth her while, but the thought of offering her money made his stomach churn. He knew he couldn't buy Kelly. Before he could fully realize what was bubbling up to the surface in his head, she stood up and Jack forced his thoughts to the side, not wanting her to read the thoughts racing through his mind.

Kelly found the pot she wanted and stood up before she noticed Jack watching her. He stared at her with an intensity that made her tingle, and she found she couldn't come up with a single word to say.

In her head, she knew "good morning" might be appropriate, but her mouth had apparently stopped functioning.

Jack silently walked to her and took the pan from her hands, setting it aside on the stove. She had about two seconds to realize she was about to be treated to another of his incredible kisses, but this time, he didn't just kiss her. He devoured her.

With his mouth still on hers, Jack walked them backward until they hit the island in the center of the room. He lifted her onto the cool granite countertop and settled himself between her legs.

This wasn't a gentle exploration of her lips. There was no feeling her out to see if she wanted him to kiss her. There was only heat and passion, so hard and strong, it made her zip to life from her belly down to her toes and stole her breath from her body.

She wrapped her arms around his neck and grabbed handfuls of his hair, fisting the dark curls as she leaned her body into his and answered his passion with her own. She didn't hold anything back with him. She couldn't. Some part of her knew he'd never take less than all of her.

Jack's hands slid down her sides and brushed the curves of Kelly's breasts, causing her nipples to tighten and peak with anticipation. As he moved lower, skimming down her hips, he pulled her more tightly to his body fitting her to him like two pieces of a puzzle.

Kelly was about to tell Jack to skip breakfast and carry her upstairs. Hell, she wasn't just going to tell him, she was going to beg, but Mabry's shrill voice cut through the kitchen.

"Well, this is cozy!"

He quickly broke away from Kelly. She blushed and buried her head in his chest as he turned to his aunt.

"Good morning, Aunt Mabry. I was helping Kelly make breakfast. It's Mrs. Poole's day off today."

Kelly looked up to find Jack wore a wide grin as he greeted his aunt.

"That's an interesting cooking style you have there, dear," Mabry said to Kelly, and for a minute with her joking smile and casual manner, she sounded like the Aunt Mabry Jack had described from long ago.

Unfortunately, the moment flashed past as her face resumed its pinched state and she stared in reproach as he slid Kelly off the counter and let her get back to work on breakfast.

Kelly nearly sighed as Jack went to the fridge where he pulled out eggs, bread, sausages, and fruit and placed them on the counter for her. She grinned at him as she started to crack eggs into a large mixing bowl and whisked them together.

"Scrambled eggs with sausage on the side, French toast with sausage on the side, or an omelet with cheese and sausage inside?" Kelly asked. She was sure there was a sausage joke in there somewhere but Mabry probably wouldn't appreciate that.

"Anything works for me, beautiful," Jack said and looked expectantly at his aunt.

Mabry scowled. "Scrambled is fine. No need to be fancy." She turned to Jack. "I saw a picture of that actress you used to date in today's newspaper. That one with the stunning black hair and the green eyes. What was her name? She was nominated for an Oscar. Kelly, you should see some of the women your Jack dated before he found you." Aunt Mabry smiled her nasty sneer as she continued.

"There were so many models, weren't there, Jack? You seem to be partial to models." She continued on.

Kelly saw Jack go still, ever so briefly, before he brushed off his aunt's words and took the bread from the counter.

Kelly knew her smile was tight as she began to pour the eggs into the heated pan and scramble them as they set. She took out another pan for the sausage while Jack popped several pieces of toast in the toaster, but she found herself blinking her eyes to hold back tears as Mabry's words sank in.

Jack turned to his aunt and then smiled at Kelly. "Until I found Kelly, I was bored to tears, Aunt Mabry. I've got the best of both worlds now. A wife who could be a model but she's funny and kind and I'm not bored to tears talking to her."

Kelly pressed her lips together and Jack met her eyes. She could almost let herself believe his words were more than a show for his aunt.

Almost.

CHAPTER 41

As Kelly and Jack walked into her mother's kitchen for Sunday dinner, Jack had the odd sensation of utter belonging and acceptance, as if he had always been a member of this family.

Kelly's brother Liam was pulling a beer out of the fridge when they entered the room. Without missing a beat, he tossed one to Jack before he cracked his own beer open. Kelly's mother kissed and hugged Kelly then turned immediately to Jack and pulled him into her embrace for kisses and hugs as if he were one of her own.

He was surprised to find himself hugging her back. Life with Kelly was starting to be one big revelation after another. When he told Mabry he had been bored by every woman he had dated before her, he immediately realized the truth of that. His life with Kelly, despite its fake beginning, was never boring. He didn't have that usual let-down feeling when he realized there was nothing under the surface of a particular woman. With Kelly, the surface was—well, it was only the beginning, just like it should be.

As Kelly and her mother finished the dinner prep, Jack and her brothers set out plates and silverware while her dad sat at the table and joked with everyone. Kelly's sister Jesse came in shortly after they arrived, and Jack found that he was happy to see her also.

The room buzzed with the easygoing chatter of the family catching up on the week's events. They all laughed easily when Kelly's mom told Jack that she looked up his company on "the Google" and was very impressed by all that he had done.

It struck him that he had always wanted this, this feeling of family. Even though he had loved his parents more than anything, and he always had Chad around growing up, he always wished he had siblings.

As he looked around, he saw the room was awash with warmth and familiarity and caring, and he wanted to spend Sunday dinners here forever.

He wouldn't. He would only spend a year as a member of this family and then things were scheduled to end. Like all this had an expiration date. And then his new siblings, new parents, would likely hate him.

They'd have to assume he'd done something wrong for Kelly to leave and all this would disappear. *She* would disappear.

Once again, Jack found himself wanting more with Kelly. Wanting to somehow erase the expiration date that mocked him every time he thought of it.

This visit to her parents' provided one surprise after another for Jack as he realized that the temporary nature of his marriage was beginning to leave a very bad taste in his mouth. He couldn't imagine resuming the life he'd had before Kelly.

Jack walked into the bedroom that evening well after nine o'clock. He had been down in his office working later than usual, but Kelly was still up reading a book in bed with the pillows propped behind her back.

He slid in beside her and laced his fingers through the soft hair at the back of her head, before leaning closer to the warm skin of her neck to trace a pattern of kisses to her jawline.

Kelly's thoughts weren't on the book for long as she turned to nuzzle against Jack and open herself to him. It never ceased to amaze her how quickly he brought her body to a frenzied state with a kiss or a touch.

Jack reached over and closed her book, putting it on the end table on her side of the bed. Slowly, he stripped her body of the tank top and pajama pants she wore.

He traced a pattern with his mouth and tongue from Kelly's shoulders to her stomach, down her legs and back up again, before giving in to her pleas. Jack quickly grabbed a condom and sheathed himself before he entered her, making her cry out his name over and over.

"God, Kelly, how do you do this to me?" He thought he would lose his mind inside her. She felt like no other woman ever had. Like she was made for him, made to fit him like a glove. He couldn't get close enough, deep enough.

With Kelly's soft pants and moans in his ear, Jack buried his face against her soft neck and plunged deep into her soft folds, rocking his hips over and over until they both cried out together and climaxed on an endless wave of pleasure and heat.

CHAPTER 42

Kelly lay in Jack's arms after they made love and thought about how content she was with the new status of their relationship. She didn't know where this was going, but she was happy for now, and for once she was just going to focus on being happy in the moment and not worry about what might happen down the road.

Jack pulled the covers up over them and wrapped her in his arms and legs, snuggling closer to her as they lay together in bed.

"How are things at the clinic?" he asked as she relaxed in his arms.

"Good. I like the people a lot, and I'm seeing a range of different legal issues. There's a new volunteer who's really nice. Denise. She's thinking of applying to law schools so she wanted to volunteer to get some experience to put on her applications. We're going to lunch so I can give her some tips on the LSAT and what she might want to think about when she puts in her applications."

"I thought law school students were supposed to be cutthroat competitors, hiding books from the other students in the stacks and vying for the best study groups."

Kelly laughed. "Well, I'm not there yet. Besides, the LSAT was kind of intimidating. I wish someone had taken the time to describe it to me before I walked in there. I would've felt better, I think."

He smiled down at Kelly. "Oh, before I forget; I have to go away for a work thing tomorrow afternoon. I'll fly out in the afternoon and be back Tuesday evening."

"Where are you going?" Kelly almost kicked herself for asking. She hadn't meant to sound like a nagging busybody wife, and she didn't really know if she had any right to ask.

He had said he wouldn't see any other women while they were together, but that didn't mean she had the right to know everything about him.

If Jack minded, he didn't show it. "Chicago. We have the right of first refusal on the sale of some shares in a company we invested in, but it looks as if the deal may be going south. I'm heading out to clean things up and make sure we get it under control before it gets out of hand."

"Do you need any help getting ready?" She didn't really know what the protocol was for a wife in this circumstance. Should she help him pack? Drive him to the airport?

Jack smiled and kissed her lips in an achingly slow kiss that assaulted her senses and had her weak in seconds. "No, but you can give me a send-off I won't forget," he said as he drew away from her lips and began to brush his mouth down her neck and across her shoulder.

He instantly rekindled the burning arousal that had been sated just moments before.

Kelly gasped in wonder, and within minutes of his hands and mouth touching her, she was ready for him again. Her body came to life and she stretched toward him with need, aching and sweet. She was beginning to realize he was the only one who could slake that need in her.

She closed her eyes and let her body sink into his, as his

hands played across her body, sending her to places she knew no other man would ever take her.

She closed her mind to the nagging voice that taunted her and told her she would never be happy with another man when her time with Jack ran out. She wasn't ready to face any of that.

CHAPTER 43

Kelly carried a pitcher of iced tea and two glasses out to the pool, where Jennie sat sunning herself on a rare afternoon off. This was the first time Jennie had been to the house, so Kelly had taken her for the grand tour before they settled outside by the pool.

Jack had already left for the airport, Mabry was out shopping, and Mrs. Poole was in the kitchen baking, so it was just the two of them for the next couple of hours.

"I still can't get over this place. I could kick myself for not thinking of proposing to Jack myself. I mean what the hell, why didn't I think of it?" Jennie laughed and picked up her glass as Kelly settled onto the lounge chair next to her.

Kelly laughed, but was shocked by the hot flash of jealousy that shot through her at her friend's words. God, she felt almost... *possessive* of Jack. She wasn't doing a very good job of keeping her emotional distance and only having fun with him.

In fact, if she were really honest with herself, she had to admit she hadn't protected her heart from him at all.

Jennie was watching Kelly's face as if she were trying to figure out the emotions playing across it. "Oh no, Kel. You're not only falling for him, you're completely over the edge, aren't you?"

Kelly felt a slash of pain as her friend spoke. "I never meant to. I didn't think this would be a problem. I've dated a lot of really terrific guys, some for a long time even. They were sweet and fun and things with them were always great, but they never really made me feel...more, you know?"

She shook her head, swamped by the hopeless emotions washing over her. "I never felt this way about any of them. With Jack, things are different somehow. I feel more comfortable with him than I've ever felt with anyone. And every time he kisses me...." She broke off as her face turned red.

"I thought I could handle it and keep my distance," Kelly went on, trying to justify her feelings to Jennie who was listening quietly, "but he's so much more amazing than I thought he'd be. Every time he takes me to dinner or we curl up on the couch, or go for a walk, I seem to fall deeper and deeper. I just can't resist him. He acts as if we're a real couple. I wasn't ready for that—you know, Jennie? I wasn't prepared to have to defend myself. My heart, I mean."

A puzzled look crossed Jennie's face. "I don't understand. If this is a phony marriage and Jack knows that, why is he doing all those things? I mean, why would he snuggle with you or take you out places? Are they things he needs to go to for work?"

"Not always," said Kelly slowly. "Sometimes we just go to dinner or for a walk. When we don't go out, we eat dinner here and sometimes watch a movie after dinner. There are times when the snuggling is for his aunt's sake, but sometimes it's just us."

"The only way that makes sense is if he likes you. If he wants more."

Kelly's eyes started to well up with tears, but she shook her head and blinked them back. "I've thought of that, but that's a far cry from falling in love with me or wanting something more at the end of our deal. Jack's used to having women around and being able to go out with anyone he wants. Obviously, he can't go out with his usual floozies during the marriage so he's taking me out. But that doesn't mean he'd want to turn this into forever." Her voice fell still as she realized *she* wanted forever.

"Floozies?" laughed Jennie, lightening the mood.

Kelly grinned at her friend. "You know what I mean."

They sat together for a few minutes and stared out past the pool and down the lawn to the sound, watching the water lap at the edge of the beach. Finally, Jennie spoke.

"Have you slept with him?" she asked.

Kelly nodded and struggled to find the right words. "I don't know how to describe it. It was more incredible than it's ever been with anyone else. And it's like we were made to fit together —like our bodies are two parts that make up a whole."

She looked to Jennie and saw pain in her friend's eyes. Jennie had known that kind of love once.

Jennie smiled but her gaze remained sad. She reached out and squeezed Kelly's hand. "Maybe he's feeling the same things you are."

Kelly thought about what Jennie was saying and sipped her tea. "I don't know if you're right, Jennie, but I do know this. I like the new me I'm becoming. I like being more daring and going for the things that I want. It started when I walked into Jack's office and I want to keep it going."

She whooshed out a breath. "So, I'm just going to grab onto this year and enjoy it with Jack. If it goes further, that'll be a bonus. If it doesn't, I'm going to have to get over it," she said with all the confidence she could muster... But she knew that getting over Jack Sutton just might kill her.

CHAPTER 44

Kelly felt wonderfully confident in her decision until a few hours later when Mabry cornered her in the living room. Kelly sat reading a book on the couch when Jack's aunt walked in.

"It won't last, you know," Mabry started in with a sneer on her face. "It starts out like this with the sudden 'business trips' and it goes downhill from there."

Kelly looked up from her book trying to dismiss Mabry's concerns. "It's just a trip to save a deal that's in trouble. I don't think it's the beginning of the end of our marriage," she said confidently.

Mabry's eyebrows shot up. She'd planted a seed that she knew would fester and grow. "Hmm. I wonder why he was speaking to Caroline Harridan before he left? I thought he was through with her, but I guess not."

The smile on Mabry's lips as she spun on her heel and left the room was smug.

Kelly knew what the woman was trying to do but it was hard not to wonder if Mabry's job was made easy by the fact Jack was really talking to Caroline? Or was it completely made up? Kelly watched Mabry go, feeling a blossoming insecure hesitation at her parting words.

She went upstairs and sat in the room she shared with Jack trying to shove aside the feelings. Jack hadn't seemed to be interested in Caroline when they saw her at lunch the other day, but if he hadn't talked to Caroline, how would Mabry know to pull that name out of thin air?

Which meant Jack must have talked to her. Could his blasé attitude toward Caroline at lunch have been an act?

Jack had sworn to her that he wouldn't be with anyone else while they were married, and Kelly had believed him at the time. He seemed so genuine and sure. But it was well known that Jack Sutton could bluff better than anyone when he needed to. Maybe he was bringing his boardroom tactics home to their bed.

Kelly hated the sudden insecurity she felt. She had never been the jealous or suspicious type when dating someone, but as she thought about it, she realized that was because she always knew where she stood with her previous boyfriends.

She had been confident in the status of her relationships in the past, so there was no need to be catty and check up on them.

With Jack, the only thing she really knew was that their whole relationship was based on a pretend marriage. A lie. Where did that really leave her?

She sat on the bed and tried to think of a way to know for sure whether Jack was with Caroline without having to flat out ask him. If she did that, he would know she didn't trust him. Worse, he might guess the secret she'd been trying to hide—that she was feeling a lot more for him than he was for her in this marriage of convenience.

She bit her lip between her teeth and picked up the phone, dialing the number of the hotel where Jack was staying. She tried to affect a secretarial tone.

When the front desk picked up, Kelly launched into her spiel.

"This is Jack Sutton's secretary. I need to reach his wife right away to confirm some details for a fundraising event that can't wait. Can you tell me if she checked in there with him? She wasn't planning on traveling with him, but I'm wondering if she may have tagged along at the last minute because I can't reach her here."

Kelly had learned that if you spoke confidently enough and acted as though you expected your questions to be answered, they often would be.

"No, ma'am. I checked Mr. Sutton in myself and he's traveling alone. Let me double check with the bellhop to see if she came later. Hold one moment, please."

Kelly waited on the line, holding her breath and chewing her lip as she waited to hear whether Jack had been joined by a woman. It was several minutes before the concierge came back on the line.

"No, ma'am. Mr. Sutton has not been joined by anyone, I'm afraid."

Kelly breathed a silent sigh of relief as she continued to play her part. "All right, I'll keep trying to track her down here. Thank you for your help," she said and hung up the phone.

She was relieved that Jack didn't seem to have Caroline with him, but that relief was short-lived when the guilt at having checked up on him kicked in. She shouldn't have done that. The nagging regret in her stomach stayed with her into the evening.

That night Kelly went up to bed early and started a bubble bath to soak. There was nothing she loved more than soaking in water so hot it almost burned, and she filled the tub with bath salts that smelled of jasmine and roses.

Kelly stripped off her clothes and sank down into the heavenly mixture. She sighed as she felt her tension begin to melt.

She had no one to blame for it but herself. She was tense because she felt as if she betrayed Jack by checking up on him, and she was angry with herself for letting Mabry get to her. She knew better than to listen to that hateful old hag.

Kelly sighed as she thought about Mabry. She knew Jack didn't want to confront Mabry because he and Chad had this overdeveloped sense of protection where she was concerned. In many ways knowing he was like that made her care for him all the more. It wasn't your average man who would put his family above all else, especially when that family member was attacking him at every turn.

Kelly took a deep breath and submerged herself under the bubbles, floating while the bath salts and hot water worked their magic. Jack's bathtub was like heaven on earth. It was large and deep enough that she could lay completely submerged without scrunching herself up, and it had excellent temperature control. Thinking that she would turn on the jets for a bit, Kelly came up out of the suds and swiped a hand down her face. Then she opened her eyes.

And screamed. Jack stood watching her come up out of the water.

"Jack! What are you doing here? You're not due home until tomorrow night," Kelly sputtered.

CHAPTER 45

*J*ack let his eyes skim Kelly's breasts where they crested out of the water as if they wanted to give him a very nice welcome home. He didn't answer Kelly's question as he honed his sharp gaze on her vulnerable body in the hot water.

She looked guilty as sin sitting there staring at him, and he knew without a doubt that it *had* been Kelly who called the hotel. He'd stayed in that hotel on a number of occasions, so the concierge was quick to let him know that someone had called to check up on him.

Jack was surprised to find he wasn't upset or angry with her as he would have been with one of his girlfriends if they had pulled that kind of crap. In fact, he wasn't even annoyed.

It puzzled him that the moment he saw the confirmation in Kelly's eyes, he felt nothing but concern for her. He couldn't imagine what had caused her to feel the need to call, but he planned to find out.

Without saying a word, his eyes on Kelly the entire time, he stripped down to nothing while she stared up at him, eyes wide, her breath now coming in short pants.

Jack kept his gaze locked on her as he stepped into the tub. He pulled her over the top of him so she straddled his lap and plunged into her tight wet heat in one deep stroke, never taking his eyes from hers.

Her legs came around his back and he buried his face in Kelly's neck as he slowly plunged into her over and over, marveling at the softness of her skin and the way her body welcomed his without question or hesitation.

"So beautiful. You feel so damned right." Jack whispered against the soft skin of her shoulder.

∽

Kelly put her arms around Jack's neck and lost herself in the feel of him between her thighs, in the way his body made hers sing with pleasure as if he had been made for her. She moaned and felt his body pour over the edge with his release, and she tumbled after him, completely satiated in his arms.

They stayed locked together…her limp body collapsed on Jack's for several minutes before they slipped from the tub, rinsed off in the shower and snuggled up in bed together.

She lay in Jack's arms for a few minutes before she realized he hadn't answered her question. She raised her head and looked into his eyes.

"You're home early."

"I wrapped up the deal and decided to come home. I missed you," he said with a grin. "Besides, the hotel said that my secretary was looking for you. She needed to confirm some fundraising details with you, so I thought I should run home and track you down for her."

Kelly let out a small squeak in his arms and he laughed. He curled a finger under Kelly's chin and tipped her head up so that she looked into his eyes. "Why did you need to check up on me, Kel? I told you I wouldn't be with anyone else, and I meant it."

There wasn't anger in his voice. Just concern.

She flushed feeling the heat she knew would be staining her cheeks scarlet when she answered. "I'm sorry, Jack. As soon as I did it I felt like an idiot, but I let her get to me."

"Ah," Jack said. "Aunt Mabry. What did she say to you?"

"She told me you were with Caroline, that she heard you talking on the phone with her making plans. I should have known it wasn't true." Kelly shook her head as she spoke. "It seemed so odd that we had just seen Caroline. I figured she couldn't have coincidentally pulled her name out of the air, so she must have actually heard you."

"Remember when I said it wasn't a coincidence that Caroline found us at the restaurant? I'd be willing to bet it was Aunt Mabry who told her we'd be there. That's the only way she would know to plant Caroline's name in your head the next day."

"And I fell for it like an idiot," Kelly said, burying her head against Jack's chest.

He smiled and began a careful exploration of her body with his mouth. He spoke to Kelly as his lips caressed her soft, creamy skin.

"I think I like that you cared whether I was with another woman. Not enough that I want you ever to worry about something like that again, but a little," he said as he kissed along the inside of her thighs.

"You don't need to worry like that again, Kelly," Jack said as he placed his final kiss in the spot she needed the most, and Kelly's moan was all the answer he got.

CHAPTER 46

That weekend, Kelly was nervous as she dressed for the party. She and Jack had been 'married' about a month, and although she had met some of his friends and business associates, she was anxious about having her friends and family and all of Jack's friends and business colleagues in one place.

It was enough to send her over the edge. She had hardly been able to eat all day, and her stomach was doing flip flops as she shaved her legs in the shower.

She finished rinsing and stepped out to dry herself. Jack had run to the office for a couple of hours, so she had plenty of time to get dressed and do her makeup.

She toweled off and applied moisturizing lotion before setting her hair. She had decided to use large curlers to give it a soft, bouncy curl for the night. Her dress had an open neckline, and the spaghetti strap style left her shoulders bare so the soft curls would flow down over her shoulders, completing the look.

Kelly applied her makeup while her hair was setting in the rollers, then slipped into the charcoal-gray lingerie she had picked to wear under her dress. She loved the demi bra that pushed up her chest and the thigh-high stockings with garter belt. She had never had lingerie that made her feel this sexy.

Smiling, she slipped her dress on over her head, feeling as if she were living a fairy tale.

Fairy tale for a year, she told herself, and commanded her heart to be okay with that deadline. That was far more than she'd ever had before this adventure had started.

Slipping into silver, strappy heels, Kelly buckled the thin straps around her ankles and walked down the stairs. She came into the front hall as Jack was stepping in from the office. He'd arrived home just before the guests were due but had changed into his charcoal suit at the office.

She smiled at the color of his suit. He had no idea they were coordinated, but she'd enjoy showing him that after the party.

Jack froze in the hallway when he saw Kelly. As he watched her, she let out a small laugh.

"That's funny that you chose charcoal," she said with all the innocence she could muster. "My lingerie is charcoal tonight."

Jack's eyes went wide and Kelly was fairly sure she heard him growl. "Damn, woman," Jack grunted and the next thing she knew he had her in a fireman's hold over his shoulder and was headed up the stairs with her.

"Mrs. Poole, greet the guests," he hollered over his shoulder as he ran up the stairs with a laughing Kelly hitting him in the back with balled up fists as he went.

"What the hell are you doing?" she cried out as he plopped her down in their bedroom, but she was still laughing.

She barely had the words out before Jack's mouth was on hers, burning into her, seeking her, finding her. She moaned into his lips as she wrapped her arms around him and melded her body to his and returned his kiss with just as much heat. She matched him stroke for stroke with her tongue and fisted her hands in his hair.

Jack broke from her mouth only to bring his lips to her neck, slowly pressing one firm kiss after another down her neck, into the vee of her dress as he softly caressed the top curve of her breasts. Kelly's head fell back and she breathed out his name, and the soft, throaty sound of her plea sent heat flaming through him.

He raised one of her arms and began to kiss her shoulder, then trailed his kisses down her arm to her wrist where he lingered on the soft skin on the inside of her wrist before he broke away and found her mouth again.

"Jack," Kelly breathed, "I need...."

"Stay," he commanded and left her against the door as he went to the nightstand for a condom.

He returned to Kelly and captured her mouth with his again before he reached between them and undid the zipper of his pants. Jack donned the condom and pulled aside the small scrap of silk and lace covering Kelly.

Lifting her, he wrapped her legs around his waist and sank into her, taking her against the door of their bedroom as their guests arrived downstairs.

He buried himself deep again and again as she pulled him ever deeper with her legs around his waist. Both reached a breathless orgasm in record time.

When they were cleaned up and dressed again, Jack crossed to his armoire and pulled a black velvet jewelry box out of one of the drawers. He opened it and turned to show Kelly a stunning set of diamond stud earrings and a light, delicate diamond necklace that complemented her dress perfectly.

She gasped and covered her mouth while Jack laughed at her reaction and clasped the necklace around her neck. He stole a few kisses on the back of her neck, but stopped himself before they reached the point of no return again.

"Jack, you shouldn't have," her hand shook as she fingered the beautiful jewels at her neck.

"I like doing things that make you smile, Kelly. I love your smile. Here, put the earrings on."

Kelly put the earrings in her ears, and Jack took her by the hand to go down to greet their guests.

CHAPTER 47

Kelly looked out across the lawn at the beautiful white tents drenched in tiny sparkling lights and filled with guests, wait staff, and a band. Out past the lawn, the water sparkled and reflected the lights back onto the party. The boat dock had been set up with tiny café tables for guests who wanted to stroll down to the water.

On the lawn, there were large round tables with white linens and linen-covered chairs set up under the tents for the sit-down dinner that would be served in an hour. She sucked in her breath as she looked out at the scene. She couldn't believe that Mrs. Poole had been able to pull this all together in a week.

As Jack and Kelly made their way down to the tables, guests stopped them. Most congratulated Jack with a slap on the back or a private toast. More than one commented that Kelly must be a hell of a woman to have caught him, and Kelly laughed and hinted at blackmail and espionage.

Andrew nearly choked on his appetizer as he walked up to greet them, and Kelly thought he must have heard her comment. She laughed as she realized Andrew was one of the few people at the party who knew how close her explanation danced to the truth. She thought she saw approval in his smile.

"Is she spreading vicious lies and rumors again, Jack?" Andrew said as he shook Jack's hand and kissed Kelly on the cheek. "If you get tired of this guy, I'm always available," Andrew said winking at her.

"Back off," Jack growled and Kelly laughed at the two men posturing. "Get your own woman, Andrew," Jack said jokingly to his best friend, but there was a hint of an edge to his voice.

"Okay, okay," Andrew said, raising his palms in defeat.

The three friends walked down toward the tents together, and Kelly felt content and happy as she greeted her own family and friends. She introduced Jack to the people who hadn't met him yet and watched him share a drink with her father and brothers.

Kelly saw Roark, the attorney she'd met in Jack's office the day they signed all the contracts for their marriage. He looked like he was trying to help Mrs. Poole as she oversaw the caterers, but she was having none of that.

"What's that about?" Kelly murmured to Jack, discretely tilting her glass in the direction of the pair.

Roark was grinning. Mrs. Poole was scowling at him in a way Kelly had only seen her do behind Mabry's back.

Jack grinned. "My lawyer has been in love with my housekeeper for at least three years. Probably longer."

"And she has a problem with that?" Kelly watched as Mrs. Poole seemed to blush and then shoo Roark out of her path.

Roark, for his part, seemed entertained by her objections, but he did as she asked and backed off. From what Kelly had seen of the older gentleman, he wasn't the type to push a woman where he wasn't wanted.

Flirt? Yes. But push her if she told him no? Not so much.

But Kelly saw the way Mrs. Poole's eye stayed on him as he wandered away and she wondered how much of his attention the woman really objected to. She'd need to remember to ask her about it later.

Kelly's family, Chad, Mabry, and Andrew all joined Kelly and

Jack at the largest of the rounds in the center of the tent for their meal. Conversation swirled from Kelly's law school plans and her work at the legal aid clinic to Jack's latest investments. At a lull in the conversation, Mabry struck out at the newlyweds again.

"So, Jack, no plans to take your beautiful wife on a honeymoon? I'm surprised you didn't whisk her away after the wedding," Mabry said too sweetly.

Kelly's cheeks flamed, and she jumped in quickly to try to explain away the unorthodox absence of a honeymoon. "Oh, with Jack's work, we can't really go running off on a honeymoon," she said.

"Actually, Kelly, I cleared three weeks in August right before you start school. I got us tickets to Italy for a week, then a week in Paris, and then to Greece before we come home. I thought I'd surprise you."

Kelly thought he must be making that up to maintain the façade of their marriage, so she was stunned when Jack pulled their airline tickets out of the inside of his suit pocket and grinned at her. Her sister squealed, but all Kelly could do was stare at him and wonder why in the hell he would do something like that.

Jack was beginning to wonder why he was doing all of these things for Kelly when this marriage was supposed to be on paper only. The truth was, he liked seeing her smile and the idea of three weeks abroad with her sounded fun.

He shrugged off the nagging feeling that there was something more going on here and focused on her smile. He leaned in to cup her face with one hand and kissed her luscious lips as she grinned and her sister continued to squeal.

Jack hadn't stepped from her side the entire evening, and his hands had rarely left her body. He seemed to want... no *need* to have a hand on her at all times, playing in small circles on the small of her back, holding her hand with fingers entwined, or running softly up her arm, over the curve of her shoulder. Jack wondered if she could feel how much he treasured her tonight.

He hoped her family was having fun. Her mother was gaga over the house, and Jack thought her father had been impressed too. Kelly made the right impression on Jack's business associates, making small talk when she needed to.

Andrew and Chad taunted him and flirted with Kelly to see how far they could go before he would strike out at them. Andrew joked that he could steal her off to a private island and whisk her away from all of this. He swept his arm out to encompass the beautiful grounds and home as if it were torture for her to live in such opulence.

Kelly laughed at them and placed her hand calmly on Jack's arm, but even that couldn't deflate the rage he felt watching them. Would it be wrong to tear their limbs off, he wondered?

Jack noticed that Chad asked his mother if she needed a ride home, and he wondered briefly if his cousin knew that Mabry was staying with him and Kelly. He would have to remember to ask Chad about that later.

Jack whirled Kelly around the dance floor. She was so light and graceful even though she claimed she rarely danced. He spun her and laughed with her and nuzzled his lips to her neck, wanting to hide her away from all of these prying eyes and hurry back to the privacy of their bedroom once again.

CHAPTER 48

Kelly and Jack said goodnight to the last of the guests and strolled hand in hand across the lawn and up to their room. He put his arms around her as soon as the door to their room shut and she laughed, open and free.

Her laughter didn't last long as Jack spun her to face him and began to string searing kisses across her shoulders and up her neck. A moan escaped from her lips and he found the zipper on her dress, pulling it down and letting the silky fabric glide to her feet.

Jack kept his lips pressed to Kelly's as he quickly lost his clothing then looked down at her in the smoky gray demi bra, lace panties, garter belt and thigh-high stockings. He let out a visceral groan as he dropped to his knees and kissed her stomach, her thighs, the soft patch of silk and lace between her legs.

He took his time, exploring her, teasing her with his hot breath over the lace of her panties. When he couldn't take it anymore, he stood, lifted her, and carried her to the bed. He laid her down on her stomach and stretched out next to her, and then licked, nipped, and kissed his way from her shoulders down to the small of her back and the beautiful curve where her back met her bottom.

"You are so incredibly stunning, you take my breath away," he whispered to Kelly as he pressed his body against her, spooning her in tight to him, her back to his front.

She wriggled herself back against his hard body and moaned in his arms.

Jack unhooked her bra and slipped it off her shoulders, then brought his arms around to the front of her, one arm to her breasts where he lightly rubbed and caressed, the other hand finding the lace of her panties where his hand slipped inside to make her gasp and beg.

"Please, Jack," Kelly said as she tried to turn toward him.

Jack refused to let her turn. "Ah ah ah. Patience, beautiful," he whispered into her ear, letting his breath tickle her skin.

Jack let his fingers play over her body as he drew out her pleasure and let it build slowly until he felt her tense, and moments later come crashing over the edge.

She convulsed with pleasure in his arms, and he quickly sought and found a condom before he turned her and plunged into her, releasing wave upon wave of the sweetest, aching pleasure as he buried himself, and found his own release deep within her.

Jack woke with Kelly in his arms, feeling better than he had in a long time. He slowly kissed her as she began to wake, and they came together again in a half-dream state and made love as the sun came up. He had never experienced a feeling like this before with another woman. He was insatiable in Kelly's arms as if he could never get close enough, never have enough of her, never tire of bringing her to new heights of pleasure.

They lay together, recovering, and Jack lazily ran his fingertips up and down Kelly's arm as she slept again. He held her for a long time and wondered at the way she made him feel, at the intensity of his feelings for her, before falling back to sleep himself.

When they awoke again a short time later, she stretched in his arms and smiled up at him.

"Shower?" she asked with a smile, and he grinned down at her.

"I'll go start the water. See you in there in a minute," Jack answered as he slipped out of the bed to start the shower for them.

CHAPTER 49

Kelly felt as if she were walking on air the week after the party. She hadn't spotted the car that had been following her all week and thought maybe Aunt Mabry was beginning to give up on having her watched.

She smiled to herself as she got ready to go to the clinic for the day. She replayed the week with Jack in her head, and laughed as she remembered how he grabbed her in the shower.

He had pressed her up against the wall and slipped his hands down between her legs to tease her. She thought he would drop her when he lifted her up, but he didn't. She'd wrapped her legs around him and he'd entered her, making love to her as the water streamed down around them.

Wednesday night, they skipped their usual movie and went straight up to bed after dinner, where Jack had stripped her of her clothing slowly, sensuously, kissing her as he went. Kelly had gasped with pleasure when she felt his mouth warm and wet between her legs, and she never stopped gasping for breath as he sucked and licked until she cried out.

She had never been with a man who was so giving before. He seemed to take such pleasure in giving *her* pleasure, in telling her how much she turned him on—and he demonstrated that in every action.

Kelly couldn't help but repay his generosity the next night when she surprised him by slipping into his home office after dinner. Jack's eyebrows shot up when she locked the door, closed the blinds, and dropped to her knees between his legs to give her husband a much-deserved break from his work.

She smiled to herself as she walked down the stairs to leave for the legal aid clinic. She went to the kitchen and kissed Jack good-bye and said good-bye to Mrs. Poole then walked out the front door. Before she could even make it down the wide stone staircase, she realized her car wasn't in the driveway. Jack's car was there and there was a red BMW convertible—but her Honda Civic was gone.

Puzzled, Kelly turned to walk back into the house, but a grinning Jack stood right behind her.

"Do you like it?" he asked.

"Like what?" Kelly asked slowly. She didn't want to believe that Jack had bought her a car. And apparently gotten rid of her car. Without even asking her.

Jack held up a set of car keys and smiled at her. "Your new car."

She leveled a stare at him. "Where is my car, Jack? My Civic?"

"I donated it to the Big Buddies Mentoring Program."

"You did what!" Kelly all but yelled, and Jack's face fell into confusion.

"Well, yeah. You won't need it with your BMW, and this is a safer car anyway. Much safer. I passed the dealership driving home and saw it and couldn't resist. I wanted to surprise you," he explained as if he couldn't understand why she didn't appreciate such a nice gesture and such a great car.

Kelly sighed as she noticed the hurt look on his face. "Jack, you can't do things like that. I have to go back to my life after the year is up, and I need my car," she said.

"You can keep the car at the end of the year," he said, and this time anger seeped into his voice. "Why would you think I'd make you give up the car?"

Kelly crossed her arms and faced him head on. She didn't honestly know why his actions angered her so much, but it felt like a big reminder of what she was; a wife who was bought and paid for, who wouldn't be needed after her expiration date.

Kelly didn't want to be reminded of that fact.

"That's not the point, Jack. I have to go back to living a normal life instead of this fairy tale. I'll be a student. And now I'm a student who has to pay to insure a BMW. And maintain a BMW. And fix a BMW if it breaks down. Did you think about that, Jack, because normal people have to think about these things? Did you even think to ask me before you gave away my car?"

She hated that she sounded so edgy and needy, but she couldn't reel the emotions back in. It was like a dam had broken and there was no sticking a finger in these holes.

"I'll pay for the insurance and maintenance for you, Kelly. I won't abandon you when this is over." Jack looked confused as though he genuinely wanted to fix things, but he couldn't fix this for her.

She stepped back as if she'd been struck. "So, I'll be a kept woman, huh? You'll put me up and pay everything for me and *what*? You'll swing by for a good lay when you feel like it?"

Now Jack stepped back. "You don't understand, Kelly. I didn't mean it like that. You know I didn't mean it like that. Maybe you shouldn't leave in a year. You can stay."

Jack said it cavalierly as if it were nothing for her to stay with him, and that's when Kelly's dream came crashing down around her. She had been so caught up in the fun fairy-tale life, in the incredible sex with Jack, and in getting to play house that she'd forgotten that she shouldn't—couldn't—fall for this man.

Because he wasn't talking about love or forever. He was just talking about a convenient extension of a lie.

Kelly's eyes began to tear up. She closed her eyes and held them shut for a long moment, willing the tears back. She knew that she was falling in love with him. She also knew that this was all a game to Jack, and once the terms of their agreement were honored, she couldn't stay with him after this year for anything less than love.

Her love was there, but there also had to be his love as well, and that wasn't what he offered.

Kelly shook her head and opened her eyes as tears began to fall.

She grabbed the keys from a stunned Jack's hands. "This isn't a game, Jack. This is my life, and you can't just tell me you want to keep playing house and expect me to stay until you get tired of this—until you don't want to play anymore. That's not fair. I have to go back to a normal life after this. I have to get past this." Her voice broke. "I have to get past you."

Kelly couldn't bring herself to tell him the truth—that she would have to find a way to stop loving him in a year. So, as the tears fell freely, she ran down the front steps and took the BMW because there wasn't any other option.

She gunned the engine out of the drive and let the tears fall as she drove to the clinic. She didn't know how, but knew she needed to find a way to protect herself from Jack Sutton and the feelings she had for him. Deep down, Kelly knew it was already much too late. She'd fallen in love with him a long time ago.

∼

Jack stood on the steps stunned at what had just happened. Everything was perfect. He was so happy. *They* were so happy. At least he'd thought they were.

Anger and frustration boiled over, and he stalked back in the house and slammed the door behind him. Hell, all he'd wanted was to surprise her, to see that smile again. What had he done wrong? Jack wondered, but he didn't find any explanation.

That incredible, sexy, luscious, funny, maddening woman was driving him out of his mind. Jack turned to go up to his room and found Mrs. Poole behind him. She looked ready to mother him and he groaned, knowing she wouldn't let him get away without saying her piece.

"Oh, Jack, dear. She's in love with you," Mrs. Poole said quietly. She wiped her hands on the kitchen towel she held and shook her head at him. "She has been for a while."

Jack felt as if he'd been punched in the gut. How had he not seen this? How had everything been so turned upside down and backward?

Jack wheeled and went back out to the driveway and got in his car. Mrs. Poole's words echoed in his head as he drove down the drive and turned onto the road.

His hands gripped the steering wheel, his knuckles whitened and his teeth clenched as he stewed over what Kelly had said to him. Jack couldn't understand why she would be angry that he asked her to stay.

They were good together. Life was pretty darned close to perfect with the two of them together so why was she so eager to leave? And if Mrs. Poole was right, and she loved him, why would she want to leave?

As Jack drove, the anger gave way to confusion and then to fear. *Does Kelly want to leave now?* No, he couldn't believe that. She couldn't be faking what they had. But, what did they have he began to wonder as he drove toward New Haven. Was she right? Were they playing house?

Damn it, Jack thought as he struck the steering wheel with the heel of his hand, it's not playing house when you're in love.

And then Jack realized the truth of it. He had fallen in love with Kelly somewhere in all of this. Once the realization hit him, it hit like a ton of bricks. He didn't want a year, or two years, or anything less than forever with Kelly. He wanted it all. Their love, a family together, eternity with her.

And suddenly he understood why she couldn't accept anything less from him. If Kelly really was in love with him, she couldn't accept an extension on their time if he didn't love her. She needed to know that he loved her too. She needed to know that it was the beginning of forever, and that he wasn't playing house with her.

But even if she loved him, would Kelly want more? She was going on to law school soon, and school and her career might not leave room for Jack.

Jack wanted to drive right over to the clinic to see her and tell her he loved her. To find out if their love was enough to build a life together. He started to head that way when he hit New Haven, but stopped himself.

Kelly hadn't wanted him to jump in and buy her a new car. She probably wouldn't appreciate him busting into the clinic and announcing his love in front of everyone.

He slowed the car as he thought through his options. He would go to work himself and talk to her tonight. He could bring flowers, open a bottle of wine on the patio under the stars, and tell her how he felt.

Jack wasn't a patient man, but he knew he needed to have patience here. It went against everything in his nature, but he made himself wait to see her. He needed to let Kelly calm down, and telling her how he felt and what he wanted, at home in private this evening, seemed the best option.

The decision made, Jack turned his car toward his office and tried to forge on with the day—when all he really wanted was to have Kelly back in his arms and secure in his heart.

CHAPTER 50

Chad knocked on Jack's office door and poked his head in. "You have a minute? I want to touch base about the tail on Kelly."

"Sure, come on in," Jack said and waved his cousin into his office.

"So, what do you have?" asked Jack as Chad came into the room and sat in one of the large leather armchairs facing his desk.

"We've seen the tail on Kelly multiple times and occasionally on both of you when you're out for the evening. My guys have run the plates, but they're expired and they rotate the plates frequently, so we're sure the registrations have no connection to the driver of the car. That makes me think this is a professional, not some crazed ex-boyfriend or stalker type that doesn't know what they're doing. We don't have an ID on the guy yet."

"I don't like the sound of that. Starting tomorrow, let's put someone with Kelly whenever she leaves the house. I want them to stay right with her. I'll talk to her about it tonight and let her know she'll have someone with her until we figure this out. I don't care if it does scare the crap out of her, I'm not taking chances at this point," Jack ordered.

"You got it. I'll have someone meet her at the house in the morning," Chad said.

"Hey, Chad...." Jack hesitated and ran his hand over the back of his neck. "Do you think this could be your mom having Kelly followed? Investigated?" he asked even though he didn't really want to bring up that possibility with Chad.

Chad's eyebrows shot up. "What?" he said and he didn't try to hide his shock. "What makes you think that? You can't be serious."

"Well, I know your mom's set on proving my marriage isn't real. Kelly's theory all along has been that your mom hired a private investigator, and she wants to ignore the tail so that they can report back to your mom that she isn't seeing someone else or hiding anything. I don't know if she could be right or not. What do you think?"

"Jack, man, I'm so sorry. I don't know why Mom thinks doing this to you is okay, but she seems to be getting worse."

Chad looked deep in thought for a few minutes before he responded to Jack's question.

"She did say she wanted to try to show the board members your marriage was fake. I guess she could've hired someone to try to find proof," Chad said, frowning.

Jack crossed his arms over his chest. "Well, I guess that shouldn't be a surprise since she's moved in with us. She does seem to be taking this pretty far."

"She did *what*?" Chad's eyebrows were practically off his head now.

Jack laughed. "She didn't tell you? I was going to ask you the night you offered her a lift home from the party. She's been with us almost from the wedding. Made up some excuse about fixing up her kitchen and not being able to stay in her townhouse or with you because you had a friend visiting. She's been living with us for weeks. I figured I'd let her get it out of her system and she'd give up."

Chad started to laugh. "Sorry, Jack, I know it's not funny, only it kind of is. No wonder she said she didn't need a ride home from the party the other night. I wondered how she was getting home but didn't press it. I guess she was home!"

Chad sobered then. "Oh God, Jack. Kelly must think our family is nuts. What did she have to say about all of this?"

Jack joined Chad and laughed at the situation that now resembled a sitcom. How had his life become like this?

"Kelly's been great about it. She barely batted an eye when your mom showed up. She didn't even object when she had to move into my room." Jack froze, realizing one second too late that he had let that little bit of information slip out.

Damn, there was a time when I was on top of every fact, every angle of a deal, and I never would have let a detail like that slip. This thing with Kelly has me a hell of a lot more tied up in knots than I thought.

"Wait.... What?" Chad wasn't laughing anymore either. He stared at his cousin. "Jack?"

Jack stood and moved to the front of his desk and leaned against it, legs crossed in front of him. "All right, listen. If I tell you the truth, will you promise not to tell your mom yet? I need some time to convince Kelly to stay with me."

"Oh, this I have to hear," said Chad, and he moved to Jack's couch and sat back with his feet up and his arms behind his head, ready for a good story.

Jack sighed and began. "Well, the day you guys met Kelly when she came to my office?" Chad nodded and Jack went on. "That was the first time I met her too."

"You met her that day!" Chad said.

Jack knew Chad was loving every minute he had Jack squirming as he told the story. He'd never let him live this down.

Jack shook his head. "That minute. When she walked in and introduced herself to you guys? That was the first time I saw her," he said and he looked more than a little sheepish.

Chad was now holding his stomach, he was laughing so hard. He sat up on the couch with his arms around his stomach, doubled over from the hilarity of Jack's situation. He seemed completely unable to talk and there were tears running down his face.

"I know, I know," Jack said. "Laugh it up. She's had me completely wrapped around her little finger since the day I set eyes on her."

Andrew poked his head in the door. "What's all the noise?"

For some reason, Andrew's presence only made Chad laugh harder, so Jack had to answer. "I'm telling Chad how Kelly and I met," he said wryly.

"Uh, the real story?" Andrew asked, and he glanced over his shoulder to be sure no one had heard him, then came in and shut the door behind him.

"The whole nasty story," Jack said with a shake of his head.

"So, he told you he thought maybe she was a call girl I hired for him? Or some random girl I picked up off the street?" Andrew said to Chad as he poured each of them two fingers of scotch from the small bar in Jack's office.

"Oh, well, I guess not all of it," Jack said wryly as Chad fell off the couch, laughing on the way down.

It took about ten minutes while Jack and Andrew drank and watched him, all the while grinning, but Chad finally got himself together enough to talk.

"So, what is she getting out of this?" Chad asked as he wiped tears off his face. Jack explained how she had found out about the will from his temp assistant and about their trade: Three years of law school tuition for one year of marriage.

"That's all she asked you for? Man, she could have taken you to the cleaners. Would have if she was anything like those vultures you usually date."

Jack nodded and laughed to himself. "I gave her my credit card and told her she could use it for anything. I looked at the statement the other day. You wanna' know what she's bought in all this time?" He paused before he answered his own question. "A dress for the cocktail party and shoes to go with it. No jewelry to match. Not two or three dresses in case she changed her mind the day of the party. What she needed and nothing more. Hell, I gave her a BMW today, and she was pissed."

Andrew and Chad shook their heads. They had enough money themselves to understand where Jack was coming from. Women often preyed upon them for their money, their positions, their power—and were really interested in nothing more. Andrew had learned that lesson in a particularly painful way several years ago so Jack knew that Andrew, most of all of them, understood how important it was that Kelly didn't care about Jack's money. Most women would have taken the credit card and run up a huge tab with no concern for the fact that it wasn't their money to spend.

"I still can't believe you got beat at your own game, Jack," Chad said as he shook his head. "You always have all the dirt on your opponents so you can win any negotiation. That's pretty amazing that she turned the tables on you like that."

Chad stopped and looked at his drink for a minute, then shook his head with a grin. "And that she had the guts to walk in here and pull that off. Man, that is one classy lady."

"I know," Jack said. "Now I need to convince her to stay with me."

"Damn, she wants to leave you already? What happened to the deal?" Andrew asked.

"No, I don't mean that. She's staying for the year," Jack said, "but I want more. I want the real thing, a real marriage, kids, her. For the rest of my life. The whole thing."

"Oh man," Chad said as he stared at Jack. "You love her."

Jack looked down at his drink and nodded slowly. "Yeah. I couldn't even admit it to myself at first, but I think I might have fallen in love with her that first day she walked in here, and it keeps growing every time I'm with her. It grows when I'm away from her too.

"The only problem is she has plans...you know? Things she wants to do, and I don't know if marriage fits in there. She has three years of law school, and that means going off for clerkships and internships and then long hours when she graduates to make her mark and build her own career. I don't know if there's room in there for me."

They all grew quiet for a very long moment, staring down at the amber liquid in their glasses and then quietly, Andrew chuckled. "Oh, how the mighty have fallen," he said in a low voice.

CHAPTER 51

Chad drove straight to Jack's house after leaving Andrew and Jack at the office. He pulled his Range Rover to the edge of the driveway and stepped out. Mrs. Poole answered when he rang the bell.

"Hey, Mrs. Poole," Chad said as he dropped a peck on her cheek. She had been a fixture at Jack's for so long that both he and Jack had begun to treat her like an aunt more than an employee. "I'm here to see my mom."

"Hi, dear. I'm not sure where she is. Would you like me to find her for you?" Mrs. Poole responded.

"No, I'll find her, thanks."

He wandered through the rooms looking for his mom, and found her sitting in Jack's living room reading the paper and drinking tea by the window. Mabry spotted him and silently put down her teacup. She set the paper aside before looking up at him.

Her expression was like that of an insolent little child who knew she was about to be scolded, but she laid her hands in her lap and greeted her son, "Hello, Chad. What brings you here in the middle of the day?"

Chad shook his head at her. He was afraid to open his mouth

for a moment. Not because he was afraid of what she might think, but because he was afraid he wouldn't be able to control himself. He had been holding back with his mom for so long, trying to protect her. There was so much built up in him, he was afraid it might all come spewing out in one fell swoop.

Chad stood with his jaw clenched and his arms crossed as he waited for his mother to say something. Unfortunately for his mother, his patience had been honed in his years as an army ranger. There was no question who would win this standoff.

His mother broke quickly. "Don't look at me like that. This marriage isn't real and you know it. I don't know where he got her from, but Kelly is a fake trophy wife to get Jack past the terms of the will. I need to show the board that...."

"Stop it, Mother," Chad spit out through clenched teeth, cutting her off mid sentence.

He'd had enough of his mother's hate and anger affecting all of their lives. "What you're doing is disgusting. It's embarrassing and hurtful and cruel. Did you know Jack has been protecting you this whole time? He stands up for you. He made sure I didn't come in and intervene between him and you. He thought that would hurt you too much and he didn't want to see you hurt. His parents always stood up for you too, but you've lashed out at all of them, over and over."

Now that Chad had started, he couldn't stop. "For God's sake, Mom. Jack's dad was your brother, and for the last years of his life and the last years of his wife's life, you treated them like enemies."

Mabry sat with a stunned look on her face for most of his tirade, but now she stood and lashed back. "You don't know," she said slicing her hand through the air in front of her son as if to strike out at the words he had thrown between them. "How dare you judge me? You don't know how it feels to have the person you love walk away as if you meant nothing. As if you were nothing.

And then to have to watch *them*. To have to see how happy and perfect their family was."

Chad couldn't believe what he was hearing. He knew she was sick, but she was acting as if Jack's parents, or even Jack himself, had something to do with his dad leaving his mom.

"Mom, stop! He left you. And that sucks. I wish to God he'd never hurt you. But you've let him turn you into this hateful person. It's turned you into a person I don't want to know anymore."

Chad saw his mom begin to falter, but he couldn't stop.

Frustrated, Chad rubbed a hand over his face. "You need to stop this, Mom. Jack loves Kelly. They're married. It's over. But more importantly, you *have* to listen to me. I don't want to be the CEO of the company. I love you, but I also love what I do for a living. I need you to hear that, Mom. I need you to respect it. Respect me."

His mother's face fell.

"I love you, Mom, but I don't love what you've been doing lately, and I don't love the person you've become. You can't do this anymore. If you can't stop, you're going to lose me. I know you've been angry since Dad left and you took that anger out on Jack's parents, and lately on Jack. It needs to stop." He walked out, leaving Mabry alone again.

Mabry sank back into the armchair and sat quietly for a long time. She tried to feel indignant. Or angry. Or righteous. But she suddenly couldn't feel any of those things.

As she replayed her son's words in her head, she knew he was right. Chad was right. *When did I become this person?* The changes in her had started when her husband walked out on her.

As she sat there and thought about what Chad had said,

Mabry realized she didn't like herself much either. Ten years later and she was still allowing him to hurt all of them, through her.

Oh God, what power I gave him. I let him do so much more damage than he deserved to be able to inflict.

It was as if she was waking up from a deep sleep and was finally able to see what was truly happening around her. The tears began to fall, and she cried for a long time before pulling herself together.

Mabry was ashamed as she sat in Jack and Kelly's living room thinking about what she had been doing. But she also knew she needed to go make it right. With a sigh, she pulled herself up and went up to her room. She packed up her bag and drove the half-hour to Jack's office to do just that.

CHAPTER 52

Jack's intercom buzzed, and his secretary announced that his Aunt Mabry wanted to see him. Jack groaned, wondering what on earth she had up her sleeve now.

He didn't know how much more of her intrusion he could take, and there was no way he'd let her chase Kelly off now that he'd figured out how he felt about his wife.

"Send her in," he told his secretary as he closed the file he had been reading.

Mabry didn't come sweeping through the door with the grand presence she usually cultivated.

Instead, she walked in as any normal person would. He looked at her for a minute and realized that, at that moment, she looked more like the aunt he remembered from his childhood.

He had missed the way she used to be.

"Is everything okay, Aunt Mabry?" Jack asked as he eyed her warily from behind his desk.

"No, Jack. I'm afraid it's not."

He looked at her face and realized she'd been crying.

"I owe you and Kelly an apology," she said, and she let out a whoosh of breath with the confession. She looked down at her hands as she twisted them in her lap, and Jack saw tears welling up in her eyes.

"I'm so ashamed, Jack. I've been awful to you and Kelly and before that, to your parents." Tears began to fall down her cheeks and she swiped at them with the backs of her hands.

Jack was stunned as he watched the transformation before him.

"I don't know how things got this bad. Somehow, you went from being the nephew I loved to being...well, I don't know, Jack. There's nothing I can say to make this right. But, I can see that you and Kelly love each other," she continued and Jack burst with happiness inside when she spoke of Kelly's love for him. Now he wanted to hear it from Kelly herself to be sure. He wanted to see if they could share a life together.

"It's all right, Aunt Mabry," he started to say, but she cut him off.

"No, it's not, Jack," she said firmly again, with a shake of her head. "I know that now. I want you to know I'm going to get help with this. I got so lost after Dan left me, and I've been angry and hateful ever since. It was like a poison washing through me. And I let it change the way I saw everything and everyone around me. Chad tried to tell me so many times what he wants and I never listened. I never saw how much my hatred and anger was hurting all of you, because I never wanted to see it.

"I want my life back. I want my family back. It's too late with your mom and dad, and I'll never forgive myself for that—for how awful I was to them—but I still have you and Chad and now Kelly, and I don't want to lose you."

Jack watched her cautiously while she continued.

"I know it'll take time to earn back your trust, and I won't ever be able to make everything up to you, but I'm going to try. I packed my things and I'm headed back over to my place. I'll get out of your hair so you and that sweet new wife of yours can enjoy yourselves without your old aunt getting in your way."

Jack laughed and came around his desk to hug his aunt, and hoped that this truly was a genuine change for her and a chance for him to have his old aunt back.

"But, I do expect invitations to dinner from time to time. And, Chad should come too. I don't see my own son often enough," Mabry insisted.

"Does this mean you'll call off your private investigator?" Jack asked and he laughed, relieved to be able to put all of this behind them.

Mabry pulled out of his arms and looked at him quizzically. "I didn't hire an investigator, Jack," she said.

CHAPTER 53

Jack felt his blood run cold and the air being sucked from the room. He gripped his aunt by the shoulders. "You didn't have Kelly followed, Aunt Mabry?"

She shook her head, pain and fear as the situation dawned on her evident on her face. "No, Jack. Oh my God. No, I didn't."

He grabbed his cell phone and dialed Kelly's number, but it went straight to voicemail.

Panic swept through him, but he pushed that down and tried to stay focused. She was probably busy at the clinic or out shopping and couldn't pick up the phone. He tossed the phone to his aunt.

"Keep hitting redial." Jack picked up his desk phone and dialed Chad.

"Chad, I need you right away. Kelly's in danger."

He hung up and looked to his aunt who was repeatedly hitting redial.

She shook her head at him—Kelly wasn't answering.

While he waited for Chad, Jack called the legal aid clinic, all the while chanting in his head. *She's fine, she's fine, she's fine.*

They told him she had left an hour ago and they hadn't heard from her since.

Chad arrived in Jack's office in a matter of seconds and Jack gave him an update.

Chad looked somber as he dialed the man assigned to Kelly. He spoke briefly into the phone then hung up to update Jack.

"She hasn't hit her panic button at all, but he's been parked on the street out front and he never saw her leave the clinic. He's headed into the clinic right now to check it out."

"I called there. They said she left already," Jack said.

"Let him check it out, see if he finds anything. In the meantime, let me get one of my tech people to your house to set up a trace, in case we get a call."

While Chad and Jack talked, Mabry stepped out the door and asked Jack's secretary to get Andrew right away. Minutes later, as Jack paced back and forth, knowing in his gut that Kelly was in danger because of him, Andrew slipped into the office and got a quick update from Chad.

Jack was cursing himself for putting Kelly in danger because the only explanation now, if someone had her...was they were after his money. If he hadn't married her, she wouldn't have been a target connected to him; there would be no reason for anyone to take her.

And, if he had taken this threat more seriously, like he should have in the beginning, she would have had a bodyguard right next to her instead of down the street. Jack wouldn't forgive himself if something happened to the woman he loved.

Chad's phone rang, and he answered it to get a report from his man in the field. His face was grim when he hung up the phone.

"He found Kelly's purse in the dumpster at the back of the clinic, and her car is still parked out front. Her phone and alarm are still in her purse," Chad reported.

"Then no GPS to track her," Jack added.

"One of the staff at the clinic said that Kelly and another volunteer named Denise took the garbage out to the dumpster on their way out this afternoon, so she left by the back door. She should have walked down the alley and around to her car out front. It looks like someone grabbed her in the back alley. She probably didn't have time to go for her panic alarm," Chad continued.

Jack felt as if he had been shot in the gut. He should have increased her security as soon as Chad found out about the rotating license plates instead of waiting to talk to her tonight. He had just found Kelly. He couldn't lose her now when he finally knew what it was like to live your life with someone else, *for* someone else, instead of being alone. He couldn't imagine his world without her.

Chad quietly doled out assignments. "Andrew, I want you to liquidate assets and free up as much cash as you can, in case we get a ransom demand. Mom, contact Kelly's family and get them over to Jack's house so we can have everyone in one place. Jack's secretary can get you in touch with a car service to get all of them, wherever they are.

"Jack, you head home now in case there's a ransom demand before I get there with tech support. I'm going to check in with some contacts I have at the New Haven Police Department and FBI. I'll be a few minutes behind you."

CHAPTER 54

Kelly's head throbbed when she woke. She felt nauseated and confused as she tried to shake the foggy feeling in her head and rid the cotton from her mouth. Panic set in when she realized her hands and feet were bound with thick layers of duct tape and she was in a room she didn't recognize.

She felt as though a band was tightening around her chest, suffocating her. Waves of panic swept over her and bile burned at the base of her throat.

She was lying on the floor in a typical bedroom, a bit small. It was daylight out. There was a twin-sized bed, and a torn-up upholstered chair in the corner, but that was it. The room was bare, other than those two pieces of furniture.

Kelly fought to pull details from her mind, grasping at threads of memory so thin they seemed to fall from her mind before she could see where they went. She closed her eyes and took a few deep breaths and pictured herself earlier in the day. It would have been noon when she was grabbed. She had left the clinic at noon.

She could remember walking out the back door of the clinic. Denise had asked her to take the trash to the dumpster on her way out, so she left through the back door even though her car was parked out front. Out front—where her security detail would have been.

She struggled to remember, but felt like there were holes in her mind, like her brain wasn't quite functioning right. She could remember someone coming at her from behind as she walked out into the alley, then a strong, sweet smell filled her nose and overwhelmed her before she blacked out. Nothing about the memory seemed right, like trying to put together pieces of different puzzles.

Tears were flowing freely now. Kelly could picture three men surrounding her, and she remembered seeing a van with two more men before she passed out. The men had worn masks....

Staying calm was no longer an option. Fresh waves of sheer terror bolted through Kelly's body. She closed her eyes tight and tried desperately to calm herself, but she had never felt a level of dread and utter anguish like this.

Her mind started running through all the ways that this could end, each image sending her into further panic until she felt as if she would choke on the fear. Then one image stopped her catapult into darkness. Jack.

Jack taking her in his arms. Jack holding her, safe again. She didn't know if Jack's Aunt Mabry was responsible for this or not, but she knew one thing. He would find her.

Kelly latched onto that image and tried to take deep breaths.

You can do this. You need to stay calm and figure out how to get yourself out of here.

She looked around and assessed the room. There were muffled voices outside the door to the room. It sounded as if all of the men were out there, but she couldn't hear what they were saying.

She did hear the sound of a television as it played in the next room. Kelly hoped that would mask any sound she made as she tried to move and release her bonds.

She stayed as quiet as she could so they didn't realize she was awake and studied her surroundings, trying to understand her circumstances. She was sitting on the floor with heavy layers of duct tape around her ankles and wrists. There was tape over her mouth too.

Thankful that they had bound her hands in front of her body instead of behind her back, she found she could use her hands a bit. She reached up with her hands and pressed her lips together to fight the urge to cry out, then pulled the tape from her mouth. She left the flap of it hanging from one corner so that she could put it back if they came in.

Kelly began to take inventory of the room.

Is there anything I can use to get out of here? Look around, Kelly. Focus.

Swallowing another wave of panic, she saw how little furniture there was in the room, how hopeless her situation was. She again forced herself to take deep slow breaths. She needed to look out the window.

Kelly lay down again and began to roll sideways, moving herself slowly and quietly toward the window. She was methodical in her movements to avoid making noise. She rolled up onto her knees, placed her bound hands onto the windowsill and levered herself up to look out the window. It had been nailed shut.

She appeared to be up on the third floor of what looked like a small apartment building. She could tell because there was another, similar building across the street, and she wondered if she could signal anyone over there but didn't see any movement in the windows.

It was hard to hold herself up at the window with her ankles bound so tightly, but she made a mental note to look out the window again every fifteen minutes to try to get someone's attention.

Kelly turned and sat on the floor, leaning her back against the wall. There were two other doors in the room in addition to the door leading to the voices. After resting for a few minutes, she rolled over to one of them.

A closet. Empty.

She rolled to the next door and opened it. A bathroom. It was as empty as the rest of the apartment. No shower curtain. No towels or bathmat. Kelly took a deep breath and rolled to her knees, put her hands onto the sink and pulled herself up. She hopped up onto her feet and bumped her lip on the corner of the sink.

She swallowed the urge to yelp at the pain and shoved open the medicine cabinet above the sink. Empty. She reminded herself to be methodical, cautious...to think.

She crouched back down and rested on her heels. *Think, Kelly, think.* That was her mantra now, to keep her focused and calm.

She looked up at the sink. It could provide a long-shot possibility; there was no other way to get out. Kelly remembered watching a child safety video when she was little. Their parents played it for her and her sister and brothers all the time. It had this cheesy caped safety hero who taught safety for kids. She had a sudden memory of a scene in the movie.

The sink. Turn on the taps and let the water run over to flood the apartment below.

She thought about it for a minute. She would need to turn it on low so the men outside the door wouldn't hear the water running. And she had to fill the safety drain hole in the basin by the wall. Balled up toilet paper did the trick. She just hoped she had enough time for it to overflow if it poured at such a low rate —and that there was someone below to see it.

She figured she could listen to the kidnappers and come turn the flow up, or try to break a window and call for help if she heard them leave the main area.

That seemed like a long shot though, because there were five of them. It was unlikely they would all leave at once, so Kelly knew her best chance was to focus on silent ways to alert others of her location. The open sink faucet might be her only shot.

Kelly turned the tap on low and plugged the drain, then rolled back into the bedroom and lay down where they had left her. She put the tape back onto her mouth and closed her eyes, and tried to picture Jack. She squeezed her eyes shut as tightly as she could and blocked out the fear by picturing herself safely in Jack's arms.

CHAPTER 55

Chad had set up shop in Jack's living room and he, Jack, and Andrew were working every angle possible to locate Kelly and get her back, but there were virtually no leads. Roark had arrived and was helping Mrs. Poole where he could. For once, she didn't shoo him away. In fact, Jack thought she might be leaning on the man for support and Jack was glad for it.

Kelly and Mrs. Poole had grown very close in the last month.

Kelly's family had been brought to the house and Mrs. Poole was doing all she could to comfort them but there was not much comfort anyone could offer them—and there wouldn't be—until Kelly was found. Her mother was as white as a sheet, surrounded by her husband and children. She was as strong as Kelly and was holding herself together as they waited for news.

Jack didn't think he had ever felt so afraid in his life. Or so angry. He had just found Kelly. They had just started their life together. He hadn't even told her he loved her or that he wanted their marriage to be real. He needed time with her. He needed her in his life.

If he got his hands on the people who'd taken her from him, he really believed he would rip them apart with his bare hands. It was a level of anger and hate he never imagined he could feel.

Chad got off the phone with one of his connections at the FBI. "Jack, it's not good news. This afternoon, four other women were grabbed, all within the span of three hours. They're all wealthy young women about Kelly's age. The FBI have been called in to all of the other families' homes. Since we haven't officially reported Kelly's disappearance yet, we can keep them out of it for now—if that's what you want to do."

Chad leveled a steady gaze at Jack as he delivered the blow. "The FBI has seen this type of kidnapping in two other cities with the same M.O. in the last year. Human trafficking is likely the only reason to grab more than one woman at the same time.

"The FBI doesn't expect a ransom call but they've set up traces at the other homes, just in case. I've got Sam here and she can trace any call that comes in here if we get one, but my friend thinks whoever grabbed the women has plans for them." He paused, as if he were wishing he didn't have to say more.

Suddenly, Jack couldn't hear anything, couldn't see anything. He was completely and totally blinded by his rage and he felt a sickening desperation. He had to find Kelly and bring her back safely.

He'd never before literally tasted hate and fear on his tongue as he struggled to just breathe, to keep going. All he could do now was to keep going, to hold on. He'd keep going until he found her.

The room was quiet for a few long seconds before Chad went on, the only sound was the wracking sobs of Kelly's mom sitting on the couch.

Her resolve had finally broken when she heard Chad's words. Jack couldn't imagine the pain she felt at hearing that her daughter had been taken like this. He desperately wanted to take away that pain by bringing Kelly back to her mother's arms.

"The FBI will likely be here shortly, but the reality is, you have the right to refuse their assistance. I recommend we work on our own instead of with the FBI. If we work with them we're constrained by the law. We have a better shot at getting Kelly back if we aren't restricted. I can use my contacts to find out everything the FBI knows and what they're doing to find Kelly, so we still get a lot of the benefit of working with them, but we can move outside the law if we need to."

Jack looked at Chad as an eerie calm moved through him and he silently vowed to get his wife back safely. "Good. That's what we'll do. Andrew, how much money have you liquidated so far?"

"Sixteen million, but Chad and I each have another seven million we can put in, and I can have another twelve million by liquidating some of our investments by tomorrow morning at seven o'clock. The rest is tied up and can't be liquidated on short notice," Andrew answered somberly.

"Okay," Jack said as he turned back to Chad. "What's our next move?"

"I've got Sam, one of my best hackers here already, Jack. She's ready to trace any calls that come in. In the meantime, she's watching chat rooms and cyber boards for any info on the sale angle. As soon as we get any information, I have a team ready to move on it. We're also going to monitor incoming 911 calls to see if anything leads us to the location of the women. It's a long shot, but someone might call in something suspicious and we'll just check out any leads."

Jack nodded, accepting Chad's plan. Even with all the financial resources and experts at his disposal, he felt helpless. And he didn't like that one bit.

Kelly watched the window as night fell. She had gone to check over and over, hoping to catch someone's eye. She couldn't call out for fear it would cause the men to come in to stop her. If they came in and saw the water flowing in the bathroom, they would know what she was up to and then she would have nothing.

The window was nailed shut, so no one would hear her

screaming at the window anyway. She lay back down and tried to rest, to wait for whatever opportunity came next.

She pictured Jack, and tried to run through every memory of every moment she could remember with him in an effort to still the fear that ran like ice through her veins.

The door to the room opened suddenly, and Kelly couldn't stop the cry that worked its way out of her taped mouth as she faced one of the men that had grabbed her. He still wore his ski mask, so she took that as a good sign that her death wasn't a sure thing. If he wanted his identity hidden from her, there was still the possibility she'd get out of this alive.

The kidnapper grabbed her by one elbow and hauled her roughly to her feet, then dragged her, stumbling along on numb legs behind him, out into the apartment.

Kelly was stunned. Not only were the other three kidnappers standing in what appeared to be a vacant apartment, but four other women sat bound and gagged like her on the floor of the room.

Four sets of wide, terrified eyes looked at Kelly. As the kidnapper who had fetched her pushed her down to sit with the other women, another one grabbed the woman closest to the other side of the room and pulled her up.

Kelly watched in confusion as he cut the tape binding her wrists and ankles and scooped up a red dress off the couch, throwing it at the woman.

He shoved the woman with the dress ahead of him as they walked into what appeared to be a bathroom. When they came out several minutes later, the frightened woman was wearing the dress and they pushed her into a room down the hall. The men proceeded this way, through all of the women until it was Kelly's turn.

She was given a black dress and brought into the bathroom where the kidnapper leered at her as she changed into the dress.

He pointed to the toilet and Kelly had the feeling that it was not optional.

She was supposed to go to the bathroom and he was planning to watch. She had been holding her bladder for hours now, but she didn't actually know if she could get herself to go with this man watching her.

She felt filthy standing there with his creepy eyes on her and she shivered as she lifted the skirt of the dress high enough to sit on the toilet and go.

When she was done, the man pushed her down the hall and they entered another bedroom in the apartment. Kelly was told to lie down on a bed in the room and pictures were taken of her. She began to have a very bad feeling that she hadn't been taken for a ransom demand and this definitely didn't seem to be related to Aunt Mabry's vendetta against her.

Porn? Could they be planning to make the women strip for porn shots to sell?

Kelly's mind raced as she tried to put the pieces together but with no food in her system and sheer terror racing like ice through her veins, her mind felt as if it were immersed in a fog and couldn't function right.

The women were brought back out to the living area to sit on the floor where their legs and arms were taped up again.

At least, Kelly thought with relief, if they kept the women out here, there was less chance one of the kidnappers would spot the water flooding the bathroom in the other room.

She closed her eyes, unable to face the panic in the eyes of the other women sitting around her and again, she tried to picture Jack's face, his arms around her, pulling her to safety.

CHAPTER 56

By eight-o'clock that night, no ransom call had come in. Sam had set up a computer to play 911 calls for Chad as they came into the system. They sat for hours listening, searching for any hint of the kidnappers' whereabouts, but so far there was nothing.

Searching for something to do, Jack turned to check with Andrew on the status of the money.

"I've scheduled a few things for the morning. I've transferred my money into your account. Chad's available funds are being transferred over to your account now," Andrew answered.

Jack held his friend's eye for a moment, and both men knew there was no need to thank Andrew for the money. No way a 'thank you' could, or would ever be enough.

"Boss," Samantha said to Chad. Chad paused the playback of the 911 calls and turned to Sam. Jack felt as if everyone in the room was moving in slow motion.

He wanted to shake them, to scream and yell until they produced something to lead to Kelly, but he knew there was nothing more they could do. There wasn't a damn lead in sight.

Sam spoke to Chad in a hushed voice, but they could all hear what she had to report. "I've got chatter on several sites.

Five women for sale. Bidding starts tonight and ends in twenty-four hours. It's them. There's a market for everything nowadays. Sometimes it's virgins or teens. They're bragging that the women are high-class socialites who, um, need to be put in their place."

Samantha winced as she said this last part, but she went on. "They said they have powerful, well-connected families so the risk in grabbing them was high, and they want top dollar for them. I can try to get us into the bidding, but it's by invitation only so I'm not sure I can manage it in time." Her eyes skittered over to Jack's face as she talked, as if she wished she weren't the one to have to report the news.

Jack's jaw clenched so tightly he thought his teeth would crack as he listened to Sam. He made eye contact with Kelly's dad who tried to hold Kelly's mom together.

Chad nodded to Sam. "Keep working on it."

He turned back to the computer and started up the 911 calls, and they all listened as calls came in reporting a lost child, kids tagging a building with graffiti, and a store alarm going off downtown.

Chad cursed under his breath and Jack's shoulders dropped. He knew if they didn't find a lead, their only hope would be to get into the auction and buy Kelly back. Since Jack doubted the sellers let anyone in they hadn't dealt with in the past, it was a long shot at best, and he didn't like long shots. He liked stacking the deck in his favor and going into things with more than one plan up his sleeve.

Suddenly, Kelly's sister, Jessica jumped off the couch. "That's it! That's her. That's Kelly."

Everyone turned to her as they tried to understand what she was saying, what she meant.

"The water leak. The call that just came in about a water leak. The lady said there was a water leak from the third floor of her apartment building and that floor is empty, under construction.

She couldn't reach the landlord, and the floor is locked so she can't get up there herself."

They all stared at Jessica, not able to understand how a water leak could mean Kelly was at that apartment building.

Jessica gestured frantically at the computer in front of Chad. "That's Kelly. Mom, Dad, you guys used to play us that safety video when we were kids." She turned to her brothers now and urgently tried to get them to remember, to get everyone to understand that Kelly could have started the water leak.

"You guys remember it. The video with that safety guy wearing the cape. If you're being held on a floor above the first level in a hotel or apartment, you turn the water on to try to flood the lower floor and draw someone up to help you. It's her! It's got to be her!" Jessica tried to get them to understand.

Jack looked at Chad, and the two men nodded at each other.

"We'll check it out." Jack said to Jesse. He gave a small nod to Kelly's father, and then he and Chad left the room and ran out the door to Chad's SUV. As Chad pulled from the driveway, he turned to Jack. "Climb over the back seat and pull up the rug in the back."

He waited while Jack climbed into the back and lifted the rug. "See that ring? Pull up on it," he instructed and Jack pulled up on the ring in the floorboard of the vehicle.

"You're a little scary, Chad. I'm glad you're on my side," Jack said as he looked down into the hidden space.

Jack pulled out two bulletproof vests, a handgun for each of them, and extra magazines. He put on the vest, loaded the handguns, and shoved extra ammo into his pockets. He held onto Chad's stuff until they pulled over down the block from the location of the reported water leak.

Chad eased the car to the side of the road and he and Jack got out. Chad took the vest and guns from Jack and put them on, then he checked his pockets for the extra clips.

"Listen, Jack. Even if we call the FBI right now, they can't get a warrant on the little bit of information we have, so there's no point in us calling them yet. We'll go in and see what we see. If it looks like they're there, we'll call in the FBI for backup. If we've spotted the women, they won't need a warrant."

Chad tossed Jack a windbreaker and baseball cap he'd pulled out of the SUV and put a windbreaker on himself. "Put this on to cover the vest in case they spot us coming into the building. We'll go in casually as if we're visiting someone and get up to that third floor."

They walked toward the building and pushed buzzers for apartments on the first and second floors. Within minutes, someone had buzzed them into the building, and they headed for the staircase at the back of the hall.

They climbed to the third floor and found a chain with a master lock on the stairwell door. The lock had been picked and the chain hung loose. They opened the door and could see drop cloths and saw horses from the construction cluttering the floor. It appeared that the construction was on hold as there wasn't a sign of workmen or any noise coming from the apartments as they walked down the hall.

Jack and Chad walked quietly down the length of the hallway and listened for anything that might give them a clue as to the whereabouts of the women and the kidnappers.

As they approached apartment 307, Jack jerked his head toward the door to indicate to Chad that he heard something. They stopped and listened closely, then nodded at one another. They heard men. Several men in the apartment talking in hushed voices.

Jack's gut told him Kelly was also in there.

They stood stock-still and listened intently for several minutes, and then looked at each other in silent communication as they backed out to the stairwell they had just come through.

Once there, Chad spoke in a hushed voice. "I count at least four in the room, maybe five. Since this floor should be empty, I can see if my friend at the FBI thinks this is enough to come in without a warrant. In reality, they have a complaint from the neighbor, so they should have a basis for at least sending a black-and-white to check out the complaint. I can probably get the FBI to escort that black-and-white. Not totally legit, but they might get away with it."

"I can't leave her in there, Chad. What if they're...." Jack couldn't voice his concern, but he knew Chad would understand what was running through his head.

"No, Jack. If they're planning to sell the women, they'll have a hands-off policy. They need them healthy and uninjured. The women should be safe for the immediate future. If we go in without any backup, we could get the women hurt instead of helping them. I know you want in there, but we have to be smart about this, cousin. We'll wait here and make sure they don't leave with the women while we wait for law enforcement," Chad reasoned.

Jack knew Chad was right, but it took all of his restraint to wait. He listened as Chad called his friend and relayed what they had found. He doubted the FBI would normally act under these circumstances, but Chad had a longtime friend in the agency who had come to rely on Chad's instincts when they had served in the military together; those instincts were well-honed and reliable.

Chad hung up the phone and turned to Jack. "Eight minutes out. Let's sit tight so we have a better chance to get the women out safely, Jack."

Jack clenched his teeth and fists. It took all his control not to run down that hall and bust down the door to get to Kelly, but he knew Chad was right.

They needed to be careful and smart to get Kelly out safely—and that meant going against all his instincts.

CHAPTER 57

Kelly sat on the floor with the other women, arms and legs bound, hoping the water seeping through the floorboards to the ceiling of the apartment below would draw enough attention to their location to bring help. Or that Jack could somehow track her here before it was too late.

It had been hours since the men took the pictures in the bedroom, and the women hadn't been moved. Several hours ago, Kelly had felt shooting pains in her legs but even those were gone now.

She couldn't feel anything in them any longer. She knew even if she had the chance to run from her kidnappers, she wouldn't be physically capable of moving much at this point.

The kidnappers had finally given the women bottled water to drink a few hours ago, but no food. They seemed to want them weak but unharmed so far.

Kelly watched as the men huddled around a computer and talked in hushed voices, and then she held her breath when one of the men went back into the bedroom that Kelly had been held in earlier in the day. *Please, please, please. Don't find the water leak.*

Kelly breathed a silent sigh of relief as the kidnapper turned to leave the room without entering the bathroom, but that relief was cut short as he froze mid-turn. Rather than walk to the door, he turned back toward the room and seemed to study the floor around the bathroom.

That's when Kelly saw it. The water was seeping out into the carpet around the bathroom doorway and had formed a darkened half-moon that gave away her secret.

The kidnapper threw open the door and saw the flooded bathroom. He stared at it for a few minutes, and she heard him curse as he put it all together and realized what she'd done.

"You bitch," he spat out as he flew out of the bedroom and hauled Kelly up by her bound wrists. He cracked her cheekbone with the back of his hand, sending pain shooting through her face and down her neck.

She fell backward onto the floor and crumpled in a heap as the pain throbbed in her cheek and tears sprang to her eyes.

The other three men whirled to face them, and the largest one immediately stopped the fist that was poised to come down on her again.

"Knock it off! We need her in good shape for the auction. No one will buy her if she's got bruises all over her."

As Kelly heard the words, her brain struggled to process them, and she finally understood. The fear she had felt earlier was nothing compared to the gut-wrenching terror that washed through her and took hold now.

She began to tremble uncontrollably, and the other women all began to struggle as their fate dawned on all of them.

"Shut up!" The larger man yelled at the women before turning to the man who hit Kelly. "What the hell are you doing?"

"She flooded the bathroom. It will have gone through to the apartment below by now. Someone will come to investigate soon and this floor is supposed to be empty. She gave us up," the first kidnapper hissed in a voice that dripped with poison and made Kelly's trembling worse.

The larger man appeared to be in charge. He began to bark

orders to the other men while Kelly lay on the floor beneath them, frozen as she waited to see what they would do to her.

"You two, go get the van. We need to move the women now. Pull around to the back door and call up to us when you're ready. We'll get the women prepped and bring them down one at a time."

The men all began to move while Kelly processed what he had said. *They're going to sell us.* With that, she felt the bile rise in her throat and it took all her strength to choke it back down.

Tears fell down her face freely now as the terror of what could lie ahead filled her thoughts, and she began to wonder if Jack would be able to find her in time.

CHAPTER 58

Jack and Chad huddled in the stairwell of the third floor and watched the hallway while they waited for the FBI to arrive. Without warning, they heard a door open in the hallway.

They pressed their backs up against the wall. Chad leaned forward and peeked through the narrow glass window in the stairwell door and saw two men coming toward them. He held two fingers up to Jack, who nodded and knelt down to cross under the window to the other side of the door.

With Chad on one side of the door and Jack on the other, they could take the men down as soon as they entered the stairwell.

The door opened, and Jack and Chad moved quickly. Each of them struck one of the two men.

The man Jack hit didn't hesitate to strike back and Jack felt the blow to the side of his head hard.

He didn't let it stop him. If he did, Kelly might be lost to him forever.

He relished in the pain the man had wrought and used it, letting his anger and hatred for him build. Jack fought back, striking at the man's head and body again and again. Then Chad was pulling him off the man.

The man slumped next to his partner where Chad had apparently gone the route of a carotid hold from the looks of it since the man lay out cold on the floor with no more than a single bruise over his left eye from Chad's first strike.

Chad pulled zip ties out of his back pocket and they bound the men's hands behind their backs.

"Let's get them downstairs before they wake up. I don't have anything to cover their mouths, and the last thing we need is for them to alert the others," Chad said.

He and Jack hauled the men down the stairs by their shoulders, letting them thump, thump, thump down the stairs. Neither was careful with their cargo and Jack would be lying if he said he didn't get a measure of satisfaction out of the fact the men would be bruised and battered when they awoke.

When they got to the bottom, they could see several unmarked cars rolling to a stop down the street, and they watched as police officers and FBI agents crept silently toward the building and came to a stop outside the stairwell entrance.

Chad looked at Jack and grinned. "Cavalry's here."

Chad opened the door to the stairwell and waived the FBI in through the door.

"They're in apartment 307. We were waiting in the stairwell and these two came out. They were both armed. I estimate two or three more inside, but I can't be sure." Chad handed over the guns they had found when they disabled the two assholes from the stairwell, and briefed the FBI agents on the layout of the building and location of the apartment.

Jack and Chad fell back and grudgingly let the law enforcement officers take the lead—but Jack would be damned if he weren't going to be right behind them. He followed silently up the stairs after them, driven by the intense need to have Kelly back in his arms safe and sound.

With the FBI in the lead and local law enforcement officers after them, the group crept silently down the hall toward the apartment. Four FBI agents framed the doorway. Two held flash grenades that would stun the kidnappers, while two more agents stood poised ready with a battering ram. Given the exigent circumstances, they could enter with force, without knocking.

The lead agent nodded his head to the agents holding the small but powerful battering ram, and they swung the ram at the door and broke through with the first swing. The two agents to either side of the door quickly threw the flash grenades into the room, and the agents stormed through the chaos and took down the two additional kidnappers.

CHAPTER 59

As the men roughly gathered the women together in the center of the room, prepping them to move to a new location, Kelly began to give up and let despair creep around the edges of her brain.

They'd watch her even more carefully now and her chances of getting away seemed even more grim than they already had. She closed her eyes as tears fell, stinging her flesh where she was bruised and cut.

She took deep gulping sobs, no longer able to hold back. She was terrified. Her mind raced as she tried to figure out how this had happened to her. How was this possible? Only that morning she'd been arguing with Jack over a stupid car. What she wouldn't give to go back to that moment and tell him she'd only been upset because she'd fallen in love with him.

What she wouldn't give for five more minutes with the man she'd married as part of a deal only to lose her heart to him when she least expected it.

A frighteningly loud crash broke the silence and Kelly watched as the door splintered off its hinges and flew into the apartment. There was a blinding light and a sound that took

Kelly's hearing completely away. For what seemed like hours—but was likely only seconds—the whole apartment was in chaos.

Kelly's sight came back before her hearing, and through the spots that floated in front of her eyes, she saw men and women. Blue vests. Guns.

Thank God. These were officers or agents of some sort.

Time slowed as she watched the officers take down the three remaining men in the room. She watched in horror as two of the men were shot while the other quickly gave up his weapon, lowering himself to the ground with his hands held out at his sides.

She and the other women stayed crouched on the floor, huddled together as chaos reigned.

Then she saw Jack.

Kelly broke, and the tears fell in an unstoppable current as Jack's arms encircled her, and she knew she was safe. She knew her nightmare was over.

He lifted and carried her, cradled in his arms, out of the confusion, down the stairs and out of the building. She couldn't hear Jack as she sobbed in his arms, but she felt his lips as he buried his face against her neck. They moved against her skin, over and over as he spoke to her, and she let herself sink into his arms while he carried her away from danger.

CHAPTER 60

Jack frowned at the doctor. "I'll have private security on her door."

He'd contacted a private security firm run by former military special ops guys Chad had recommended. HALO Security had people on the way already.

The doctor seemed like he might argue, but Jack's look stopped him. No way in hell was Jack taking any chances. The kidnappers had been arrested at the scene, but this had to go further than the men who'd been in that room.

He looked over to the bed where Kelly slept. She had bruises on her face and abrasions on her wrists, and she was being monitored in case she went into shock.

He wanted to growl every time anyone went near her. He didn't care if these were the doctors and nurses taking care of her. He was in full-blown protection mode.

The FBI had questioned her, but Jack didn't let that go on for too long. As far as he was concerned, they could postpone the rest of their questions for a day or so. They had enough to track down with the men they'd arrested and the computer they'd confiscated at the apartment.

He got his way. They'd agreed to question her after she had a chance to rest.

The doctor left and Jack sat next to the bed, looking at the face of the woman he loved. Battered and bruised, she was still the most beautiful woman he'd ever seen. He didn't know if she'd want to make this marriage real, but he was going to do everything he could to show her he loved her. He wanted to spend the rest of his life by her side.

The door opened and Kelly's mom and dad came in, followed by her sister and brothers. He stood, moving to the side as they hurried to the bed. Kelly didn't stir.

"They gave her a sedative," he whispered. "The doctor said she'd probably sleep for most of the day."

He didn't know how Kelly's family would feel about him right now. It was his fault their daughter was lying in that hospital bed. If he hadn't married Kelly, no one would have had a reason to target her.

Would they hate him? Wish Kelly had never met him? Would they push Kelly to run far and fast from him?

Mrs. Bradley turned to him and her next words answered all his questions. "Come here, Jack."

She opened her arms and pulled him in, and damn if he didn't want to cry right there.

"You brought her back to me."

Kelly's mom was crying, he realized.

Mr. Bradley came over as soon as his wife released Jack from her hold. He offered his hand. "You're officially my favorite son-in-law."

Jack grinned, feeling hopeful for the first time in hours. "I'm your only son-in-law."

Kelly's mom moved back to the bed and brushed the hair back from Kelly's face.

Her father again. "Mrs. Poole and the others are out in the hallway. I should give them an update."

"I'll go," Jack said. He didn't want to go too far, but he wanted to check to see if the security people had arrived.

He was immediately pulled into another hug as soon as he left the room. Mrs. Poole's arms enveloped him in soft warmth and he took a minute to let himself sink into it and soak it up.

When he pulled back, it was obvious from the expectant looks that he'd better start talking or else. Chad, Andrew, and Mabry were waiting for answers.

"She's okay. Bruised, and they want to keep her for observation, but she's fine. She's sleeping."

As he said the words, the strain of holding it together hit Jack all at once. He let his back slide down the wall and he landed, sitting on the floor as his hands started to shake uncontrollably.

He'd almost lost the woman he loved. The person who mattered the most to him in all the world.

Jack held Kelly as she slept. She'd come home the day before, but he'd had a hard time convincing himself she was there to stay. She had slept most of the time she'd been home, and he'd stayed by her side or held her most of the time.

Of course, since he had yet to talk to her about how he felt, it wasn't actually a sure thing that she would stay. She might not feel the way he felt. She might not love him the way he loved her.

He felt his love for her grow stronger and bigger with each moment that passed. He saw their future together as he watched her sleep. A home, children, grandchildren—together. To come so close to losing her scared him to death. It was time for him to tell her how he felt.

As he watched, Kelly's eyes fluttered open with the rising sun. She turned to him and smiled, and that smile made him feel like his heart would burst.

"Hi," Jack said quietly to her.

"Hi," she said back and rested her head on his chest silently for a few minutes. Then, "I was so scared, Jack."

"I know, sweetheart. I've got you now, and I won't let anyone hurt you again." He held her tight and pressed his lips to her temple. "Kelly?"

"Yes, Jack?"

"Please don't ever leave me." He took a long slow breath. "I love you, Kelly. I love holding you. I love laughing with you, arguing with you, and just plain being with you. I love the way you accept everything about me without trying to change me. I love making love to you and holding you when you sleep. And I don't ever want to give that up. Not in a year, or two years, or ever. When I'm with you, I know I finally found the kind of love my parents had—the kind of love that will last forever."

She gasped and raised her head to look at him with tear-filled eyes.

He looked into her eyes and saw his answer there, clear as day for him. "Will you marry me, Kelly?" he asked.

When she laughed, he added, "For real, this time? Marry me, again?"

Kelly laid her head back down on his chest as though he wasn't holding his breath. As though he hadn't just asked her the most important question of his life.

"Yes, Jack. I'll marry you for real."

EPILOGUE

Over the next few weeks, they began the process of trying to put the turmoil of the kidnapping behind them. The kidnappers were arrested, and their testimony led back to the mastermind of the human trafficking ring.

Denise had been planted in the non-profit Kelly was volunteering at to befriend Kelly and get close to her. She had set up Kelly by getting her to go out the back door so her security detail wouldn't know she was in trouble until it was too late to do anything about her disappearance.

The group had struck previously in two other cities, and the FBI was working with the kidnappers to have their sentences reduced if all ten of the other women who'd already been sold could be located and returned home.

Samantha was working to help police locate and monitor the people who accessed the site where the women were sold in the auctions. A sting was being set up to arrest interested buyers.

HALO security was staying on Kelly until she felt safe being on her own again, and she was going to take some self-defense lessons and see a therapist to help her regain her confidence.

Kelly felt good that she had taken steps to help Jack and the police track her down, but she still felt vulnerable when she left the house, and she knew she couldn't live her life feeling that way. She needed to take back what those men had taken from her.

She knew that Jack would help her do that.

Jack and Kelly planned to renew their vows in a real wedding ceremony the day before they left on their three-week trip in August.

Jennie and Jessica helped Kelly pick out the wedding dress of her dreams and pale violet bridesmaid dresses for them to wear.

Chad and Andrew would stand with Jack as his groomsmen, and Aunt Mabry would sit behind Jack where his mother and father would have sat. Chad and Jack agreed; it was good to have Mabry—the old Mabry—back among them.

Jack walked into the house and called out for Kelly and Mrs. Poole. He had come home early from work, something he had been doing a little more often since Kelly had come home from the hospital. Mrs. Poole came bustling in from the kitchen.

"Hi, Jack," she greeted him with her usual cheery smile. "She's sitting outside on the patio. She seems more relaxed today."

"Thanks, Mrs. P. What's for dinner?" he asked as he kissed her cheek.

"Roasted chicken with new potatoes and carrots," Mrs. Poole answered as she swatted him away and shooed him in the direction of his wife.

Jack watched Kelly for a few minutes as she sat in one of the Adirondack chairs on the patio. There was a book next to her but it sat on the table unopened, and he hoped she wasn't thinking about the kidnapping. He would do anything to take away those memories and help her heal.

Jack thought back to his life before Kelly and wondered how it was that he hadn't known how empty his life was. He had no idea until she arrived that he was missing the fullness of a life with the one that he loved. As he crossed to her now, he thought of the completeness he felt with her by his side.

"Hi, beautiful," he said as he came up behind her. He was

happy to see that she didn't flinch when he spoke. He pressed a kiss to her lips and sat on the edge of her chair and looked into her eyes.

"What are you doing out here?" Jack asked.

She smiled at Jack. "I was just looking at the lawn and thinking that this is a lawn that is calling out for children. I'll be busy with school for a few years, but I want us to have kids someday," she said as she looked out over the lawn. "There should be children splashing in the pool and children running down to the beach. There should be a dog and a tree house. And a horseshoe pit. We should have horseshoes."

He grinned. "Anything you want, sweetheart, as long as I have you. Anything you want," and he gathered his wife into his arms and swept her away into the fairy-tale land of kisses and passion once again.

Two days later, Jack walked down the hall of Sutton Capital toward the lobby. He was hoping to catch Andrew when he came in so they could grab coffee before their mid-morning finance meeting.

He was still smiling. He hadn't really stopped over the last couple of days.

Having Kelly in his life for real—knowing that she was there because she loved him as much as he loved her—changed everything in his world.

He still loved his work and valued the company he ran, but all of it meant more to him now. The future meant more to him, knowing he would share it with her.

As he came into the lobby, he saw Debbie, Andrew's secretary, watching the elevator doors shut. He caught a glimpse of Andrew in the elevator, and something hadn't looked right.

"Everything okay, Debbie?" he asked.

She turned and the look on her face told him it wasn't at all okay. "His grandmother took a bad fall. She's on her way to Yale-New Haven right now."

Jack bit back a curse. Andrew was close to his grandmother. This was going to be hard for him. "Any news on her condition?"

Debbie's expression was tight and grim. "It's possible she broke her hip. That's about all I know so far."

"Keep me posted?" At her nod, he continued. "And let him know he can take all the time he needs."

Jack watched the elevator, helpless to do anything to help his friend.

---The End---

Thank you so much for reading! I hope you fell as hard for Jack and Kelly and all of the Sutton family as I did when I wrote their story. In fact, I didn't want to stop and I hope you don't either. Sexy Andrew Weston gets his story next. It's hot and oh so steamy with a side of suspense to keep you on your toes! Grab Reuniting with the Billionaire here and binge now! loriryanromance.com/book/reuniting-with-the-billionaire

Read on for chapter one of Reuniting with the Billionaire:

CHAPTER ONE

Jill Walsh groaned as she watched the tan Jaguar pull up her driveway and park behind the moving van.

Crap.

She rolled her head backward, to the left, then the right. Slowly, slowly, trying to ease the tension from her body. It didn't work. Her teeth seemed welded together as her jaw refused to unhinge.

Are you kidding me?

Jill didn't bother to approach the car. If Jake insisted on coming today after she told him not to, he could damn well get out of the car and come to her.

Another groan escaped Jill's lips as Jake opened the car door and did just that.

"I told you not to come," Jill said not looking his way. She continued to watch the movers as they carried out the larger pieces of furniture. Most of the furniture would go into storage since her grandparents' home, which she would be living in temporarily, was already furnished. Only her photography equipment, her clothes and a few personal items were going to Westbrook with her.

"I thought I should be here. Just in case you need me," Jake answered with that pitying little smile on his face.

It irked the hell out of Jill that she still had feelings for her ex. That even though Jake treated her like a two-year-old, and even though he'd left her for his mistress after seven years of marriage, and even though he was an obnoxious jerk who just couldn't leave her alone, a part of her still wanted to rewind the clock and go back to the way things were before Jake told her he wanted a divorce.

Jill didn't answer him. It was a waste of breath. Clearly, if he listened to her, he wouldn't be here right now.

"Ma'am, you said there were things upstairs you're setting aside for Goodwill? Do you want to show us what to leave for them?" asked one of the movers.

"What? She's not giving anything away," said Jake. He stepped between Jill and the mover.

Jill gritted her teeth, her breath bursting out as she stepped around Jake.

"Yes, Jake. I am." Jill turned to address the moving man who now looked uneasily back and forth between Jill and Jake.

"All of the furniture in the master bedroom is going to charity. Can you move it downstairs, please? They're going to come take it after we finish up here," Jill said.

"What? Why are you giving the furniture away? It's perfectly good. I gave you the furniture so you wouldn't need to get anything. I'm trying to take care of you and you're giving it away?"

He loved to sound like the hero in the divorce settlement. A big man, taking care of poor little Jill.

She closed her eyes and began to count. *One…two…three… Oh to hell with it.*

"Yes, Jake. I'm giving away the damn furniture," Jill said, rounding on him as the movers retreated back into the house, away from the awkward tension of watching strangers argue. "Do you honestly think I want the bedroom furniture? That I would sleep in the bed where you slept with her?" Jill swallowed hard as she tried to finish the sentence that stuck in her throat.

Jake didn't look the least bit chagrined. "It's perfectly good furniture, Jill."

"You're unbelievable, Jake." For what felt like the tenth time since Jake arrived only a few short minutes before, Jill closed her eyes, took a deep breath and tried to center herself. Tried to let the feelings wash off her. Tried to release the tension.

"I'd like you to leave, Jake. I asked you not to come here and I'd like you to leave," Jill said, her eyes still closed.

"I just want to help you." He was indignant, as if Jill were being insensitive to *his* needs.

She opened her eyes and leveled a shuttered stare at him. "I need you to leave. I need a clean break, Jake. I need you to leave me alone and let me move on. You've clearly moved on with Missy." The name felt like acid coming out of Jill's mouth. "Let me move on."

She wrapped her arms around her body, hugging herself tight

and turned back to watch the movers bring the last few boxes out of the house she'd shared with the man she'd loved with all her heart.

When the sale of the house had gone through yesterday, she had finally been rid of the last piece of communal property. She now needed to be rid of the memories and the heartache. Distance herself from her failed marriage. From the feelings she couldn't seem to get away from.

It was several more minutes before Jill felt him move away. She really didn't understand what he wanted. Why come around if he didn't want to be married to her anymore? Was it guilt? Control? Was he trying to keep her waiting in the wings in case he changed his mind?

She didn't understand his motives and didn't care at this point. In the beginning, his continual presence had given Jill hope. Now, she didn't want hope. She wanted this over. Over and done with for good.

A moment later, she heard his car start, listened to it as it pulled down the driveway. She began her neck rolls again. Slowly rolling back, left, right.

Breathe, Jill. Back, left, right.

Nope, didn't help a damn bit.

Get Reuniting with the Billionaire here!
loriryanromance.com/book/reuniting-with-the-billionaire

STALKER NOTES (OTHERWISE KNOWN AS AUTHOR NOTES)

I call *The Billionaire Deal* my virgin book, because it is literally that. It was first published in a shorter form under the name *Legal Ease* and was the first book I ever wrote. It was what started me on this insane journey I've had the pleasure of being on for seven years. I'm so glad you found it.

I knew I wanted to write a marriage-of-convenience book, but I didn't want it to be the standard rich man asks girl to marry him for money kind of thing. I wanted a twist. I also wanted a strong heroine, because who doesn't love a strong woman!!! Kelly stole my heart when she walked into Jack's office and proposed by sticky note. I hope she stole yours as well.

If you loved *The Billionaire Deal* and want to read more about the lives of the people at Sutton Capital, send me your email and I'll send you *Reuniting with the Billionaire*, book two in the Sutton Billionaires Series, free! Visit loriryanromance.com/penalty-follow-up.

ABOUT THE AUTHOR

Lori Ryan is a NY Times and USA Today bestselling author who writes romantic suspense, contemporary romance, and sports romance. She lives with an extremely understanding husband, three wonderful children, and two mostly-behaved dogs in Austin, Texas. It's a bit of a zoo, but she wouldn't change a thing.

Lori published her first novel in April of 2013 and hasn't looked back since then. She loves to connect with her readers.

For new release info and bonus content, join her newsletter at loriryanromance.com/lets-keep-touch.

Follow her online:

 facebook.com/loriryanromance
twitter.com/Loriryanauthor
instagram.com/loriryanauthor

Made in the USA
Monee, IL
31 January 2021

59147446R00142